I, Anupam

Nabaneeta Dev Sen

Translated from Bengali by

Paulami Sengupta and Tias Basu

with the author

THORNBIRD

NIYOGI BOOKS

Published by
NIYOGI BOOKS
Block D, Building No. 77,
Okhla Industrial Area, Phase-I,
New Delhi-110 020, INDIA
Tel: 91-11-26816301, 26818960
Email: niyogibooks@gmail.com
Website: www.niyogibooksindia.com

Editor: Sukanya Sur
Design: Shraboni Roy

ISBN: 978-93-86906-86-1
Publication: 2019

Printed at: Niyogi Offset Pvt. Ltd., New Delhi, India

ONE

Must go back now.

He raised his left wrist, hidden beneath Kamalkali's ruffled hair, and checked the time—it was nine-thirty in the morning. He had an appointment with Ambar at ten. The draft for the legal aid committee must be prepared today.

Right hand on the steering and the left busy with Kamalkali, he gently pecked her on the orange lips and said, 'Let's go back. What do you say?'

'So soon?'

'Someone is supposed to come at ten.'

Kamalkali made a pout and shot a preying glance. But knowing that she was not akin to a bird, she arranged her saree and sat up.

'You have time for everybody in the world except for me.'

He smiled and nuzzled Kamalkali a bit. When he smiles, his demeanour undergoes a sudden change—quite unexpected. This sudden flash of innocence in his childlike smile does not match with his otherwise solemn personality. It increases his attractiveness nonetheless. His right canines are cast in gold; they developed cavities when he was a child. That's why he does not laugh often. The pair of golden teeth embarrasses him.

'This is unfair. Same old eight to nine-thirty. And you are complaining that I do not have time for you?' His voice had a heady element. She could not get over him. Her lips continued to pout like a budding sweet pea flower.

'Has anyone ever seen me wake up at seven-thirty in the morning just to take a walk in the Maidan? But I have made possible such impossibility only for you, and now you are complaining....'

Kamalkali's enticing smile radiated—from her eyebrows to her chin. He now tried to concentrate on the road. His left hand was still on Kamalkali's shoulders. It had to be removed; the gear needed to be changed. He held on tightly to Kamalkali's bare rounded shoulders, flourishing beneath a sleeveless piece of apology for a blouse. He would now loosen his grip and hold the cold and hard gear instead. Anupam is well versed in such lessons of love, and so is Kamalkali. This is why he is fond of women like her. They are with you only when they are with you physically. Once they are off, their thoughts do not chase you to your bedroom, bathroom, or study. They do not encroach upon your being or your time. He does not like the other kind. The moment he comes across women showing such symptoms, he becomes alert and brushes them off his coat like monsoon insects. Not that there are no exceptions. Some girls, such as Maria and Sudha, have the tendency to spread all over your life like powdered chalk. Brushing them off requires extra time. But it is nice to be with women once in a while.

A quiet shelter away from the heat or the storm. A minute's tryst with loveliness. Just this. He has a lot of work and holds various responsibilities. His time is precious.

Like the whole world, Kamalkali was also aware of his extremely busy schedule. It made her quite conscious of her recent stroke of luck. Of late, she was seen accompanying this highly important person to a lot of places. She was getting driving lessons from none but the famous Anupam Roy. You just need to drop his name in a room filled with people; it works like a matchstick in a can of petrol. He has attained nationwide fame since the Indo-China War. He is a columnist with *Daily News*, the only English newspaper that is published simultaneously from three metropolitan cities in India. His weekly column, titled 'Roy's Corner', carries political analyses. The sales of *Daily News* had skyrocketed in Delhi and Calcutta as soon as 'Roy's Corner' was introduced. That's how the Bombay edition came up—due to the popularity of his writing. Now the paper has spread its roots into these three cities. These events have become a legend in the world of journalism. 'Roy's Corner' is also a weekly national programme on All India Radio. Anupam Roy gives an update on world politics for six minutes. Everyone is acquainted with his deep baritone voice and perfect English diction. During the Bangladesh War, *New York Times* published his war reports every day. He has been interviewed by three American television channels and by BBC.

But it would be wrong to say that he is famous only as a political analyst or a political commentator. Anupam Roy made his mark in the world of academics much before the Indo-China War commenced. For the past seventeen years, he has been engaged in setting up a new department in the university, that of Comparative Politics. He has firmly resisted the countless invitations of becoming the vice chancellor of various universities, refused government ranks as well as plush job offers from abroad. He has not budged from his native land or his values. Dr Anupam Roy does not run after excessive money or power. He has followed a basic principle in all spheres of life. Even girls like Kamalkali know that in this opportunist's world, it is very difficult to stay away from the temptation of being powerful and famous.

The Department of Comparative Politics has gained global reputation by dint of Anupam's solitary efforts. He also takes a few postgraduate classes on journalism. Students from various departments attend his classes. Besides being a good writer, he is an excellent orator too. The grapevine says that Anupam Roy might be awarded the Padma Bhushan* the next Republic Day. His news analysis during the Bangladesh War earned him international fame; the government is rewarding him for his outstanding contribution to journalism. Rumour mills are always abuzz about this man. Kamalkali does not know what to believe or not believe about him. She does not understand morality; she only knows that whatever Anupam Roy does is correct.

They had almost reached her residence. Kamalkali quickly ran her eyes over the surroundings—who all could see her as Anupam Roy's arm candy? How many enthusiastic and curious eyes had noticed her enviable status?

* The third-highest civilian award in India.

It was nine fifty-three now. Ambar would come at ten sharp. Bending down, Anupam opened the door for Kamalkali and said, 'See you.' 'When do we meet tomorrow?' 'At eight fifteen?' 'Fine.' 'You won't forget, right? Should I call and give you a reminder?' Anupam laughed again, 'Na. I am not a forgetful teacher. I remember everything. See you at eight fifteen tomorrow.'

Anupam Roy is seldom late for an appointment, let alone miss one, unless there is an insurmountable problem. He has never missed the bus in life. He has always maintained discipline. He indeed uses his watch to keep track of time and it is to people like him that you can gift a diary. However, looking at this quiet cheerful man, you will never gauge that he is ever in a hurry.

As Anupam started the engine, he looked at Kamalkali's hand, which looked straight out of a photograph, waving him goodbye against the blue background of the sky, framed by the greenery of her lawn. Were those hands trying to catch a flying bird or wanting to set a bird free? It was five minutes to ten now. There was plenty of time; his house was just three minutes from here.

TWO

He was chatting with barrister Ambar Mukherjee over coffee. Something needed to be done—a legal aid committee must be formed. The committee would not have any connections with any underground organizations. They were trying to start an urban group for protection of civil rights, funded by common people. This was being done with the aid of a few lawyers, hence, lawfully. More than 2,500 boys were behind the bars without legal proceedings. They were ageing prematurely due to unbearable torture. Those who were dying were dying, but the ones who were alive had to be protected. A central committee needed to be established. A list of lawyers, who could offer help, had been prepared. Now they would have to concentrate on the collection of funds.

In the midst of the conversation, he got a call, a reminder regarding a meeting in the evening. He possibly did not need this—it had been listed in his diary. For him, checking the diary is as regular as his daily habits. Meetings and meetings. There is some meeting or the other every day, and then there are parties. Anupam's life is crowded with people, but amidst the crowd he is solitary and free. Totally free and alone. Even if he meets numerous people, his solitude remains uninterrupted, his freedom is unhurt. Just as ducks' feathers remain untouched by water, Anupam can maintain his serenity even in the crowd. His thoughts remain organized, his memory does not fail him, and his nerves stay alert, irrespective of the multiple situations or crowd he encounters daily. He is skilled at polite conversations and humane behaviour. No matter how uninteresting the topic of discussion is, he manages to look pleased. The anger at the tip of his pen articulates itself artistically in his column—'Roy's Corner'. He never loses his cool. Apart from a handful like Hitler and Stalin, very few people have managed to earn his hatred. Human beings are earthly creatures and are naturally weak; Anupam knows it so well. It is so natural for people to be deceitful and mean, just like flaws and confusions.

He received three telephone calls while talking to Ambar. The first one was the reminder regarding the meeting in the evening. The other call was from his younger brother Nirupam. Nirupam was supposed to drop their mother at Anupam's place today, but it was not happening as he was unwell. If Anupam could manage to drop by after his university classes in the evening, he would pick her up; otherwise Nirupam would bring her the day after tomorrow. The third caller was Mohan Rao from the Reserve Bank. There was a gathering at his place in the evening. Parthasarathi had come to the city to attend a directors' meeting of Citibank. A dinner had been arranged to meet him. There was a registered letter, inviting him to a seminar in Chandigarh. Then there came a telegram—a request to be a part of an interview panel in Bombay. Keshto had left a few more letters at his desk. One handwriting was familiar—Sudha's letter.

In the midst of all this, Anupam, along with Ambar, managed to prepare a draft for the legal aid committee, its objectives and plan of action, a list of proposed members for its central committee, and the minimum target for the collection of funds.

Ambar Mukherjee's work was over. He had stood up to leave, when there were three knocks at the door. Three distinct knocks. It was repeated after a moment's pause. Keshto—Anupam's smart, young help in printed Hawai shirt, tapered pants, and Bombay-style sideburns—looked at him questioningly. After Anupam nodded, Keshto went to open the door. Now it was Ambar's turn to look surprised. He looked up. The fan was on, so that meant there was no power cut. Then why was the visitor knocking instead of ringing the bell? 'Samir,' Anupam said with a smile.

A tired, young man of about twenty-two, with unkempt beard and hair, wearing dirty kurta-pyjamas and a pair of black, thick-rimmed spectacles, entered the room. A sense of embarrassment was clear on his face when he saw Ambar inside.

Anupam assured him, 'Barrister Ambar Mukherjee. You must have heard about him.'

Relaxed, Samir smiled and folded his palms together to greet Ambar. Then suddenly, he called out, 'Keshtoda,* can you get me something to eat?'

Keshto replied from the kitchen, 'I will give it just now, Samirda. Dadababu, take your bath.'

---

* Short form of 'dada', meaning elder brother; also an informal and affectionate way of addressing men, often irrespective of their age.

Samir stretched his legs on the floor and asked Ambar as he was on his way out, 'Is there any news of Jaideep's case? I heard Gora will be released on bail. Is that true?'

Ambar turned around and said, 'Gauranga Mitra has been released yesterday. I do not see any hope in Jaideep's case. Babul has put them in trouble. We are still trying. Let's see.'

Anupam saw Ambar off, had a quick bath, and sat at the table with Samir. He had coffee with Ambar; it would be good to have some cold beer now. But Samir did not touch all this. Should he drink alone? No, let it be.

Digging into the mound of rice, Samir said, 'Anupamda, I landed myself in trouble. The tutorial home where I used to put up at night has been raided yesterday. Good that I got to know about it on the road itself and managed to escape by luck. They arrested Debu and Badal. Can I sleep here tonight?'

Anupam weighed the pros and cons as he picked at the fish bones. He could not let Samir stay for the night here if his mother came today. Ma would ask questions. Keshto knew and understood these—he was safe. Ma would not understand. But where would poor Samir go? The police were chasing them boys at every nook and corner. Let Ma be in Darjipara today. Nirupam could drop her here the day after, like they had discussed.

'Fine. You can stay here tonight, but my mother is coming the day after tomorrow. Will you be able to make some other arrangement before that?'

'Day after? That's a long time,' Samir smiled warmly and squeezed a slice of lemon into the dal.

Anupam has done a lot for Samir. Not only Samir, he has also helped Badal, Dipu, Ashok, and Debashish, with advice, with funding, and with his position. At the same time, Anupam is basically a peace-loving man. The idea of peace being restored at gunpoint gnaws at him. As a member of the Roy family, his blood is somehow not comfortable with bloody politics. On the other hand, his mind agrees to the leftist idea of revolution. Blood and reason hardly blend in today's world. Anupam has realized that there is nothing to be surprised if your reason and blood do not match. He does not indulge in what his blood insists. Civilization means the victory of reason over blood.

Anupam writes his prose freely. This is a major evidence to the fact that the country is free. Though democracy in India is disabled, it is still in good health. As a political analyst, Anupam is aware of the power of his little Mont Blanc pen at this moment. Its power knows no limits. Leaders of all the political parties are dead scared of his pen. He is equally revered by the prime minister as well as by the leaders of the opposition party. After meeting the Royal Bengal Tiger over breakfast, Anupam has lunch with lambs from Kamakhya; he eats his dinner at Gir with the lions and drinks beer with nilgais at the Vindhya Mountains. Since he loves to see himself as an idealistic and virtuous man, he does not believe in misusing his power. It is possible to change the direction of politics just by wielding his pen. The pen has the ability to affect the general mindset—Anupam knows this well, and so do all the politicians. However, Anupam

Roy is honest and courageous. The biggest trouble is that he is not greedy. For him, there is nothing to offer but dry fame. Nothing can be done.

His prowess is not limited to politics. Mr Ramsharan Agarwal, the general manager of *Daily News*, which is a rival of *Daily Star*, has been wanting to buy him an apartment at a place of his choice. His paper also circulates from Bombay, Delhi, and Madras; Anupam is free to choose. In return, Anupam would just have to write in the *Daily Star* instead of *Daily News*. Anupam refused. He could never adjust to *Daily Star*'s editorial policy.

Anupam will not trade his freedom for an apartment. When the director of *Daily Star*, Sir Raghavan, had encouraged Ramsharan Agarwal to approach Anupam to take charge of the paper, Agarwal had done so and was ready to pay Anupam as much as he wanted. *Daily Star* just had three conditions: Anupam will not be able to write anywhere else; he will not take up any other job; and his column should align a little more towards the centre. Anupam will not have to support the right, but he should not lean towards the left of the Himalayas. He could very well beat the government's left! Anupam wore a humble smile and said, 'Thank you, Ramsharanji, but I am actually a teacher. If I let go of this occupation, I will be like fish taken out of water.'

Ramsharan Agarwal has continued to visit him after that. He still comes to Anupam's flat with a bottle of Chivas Regal or Rémy Martin. Anupam really tries to stick to his ideals. His behaviour is egalitarian. He is equally polite with his students, colleagues, and office-bearers, as well as with his friends and family members. Yes, he is equally nice to his family—unlike other intellectuals who ignore their families. Everybody in his ancestral home unanimously feel that there can be no one as good as Anupam.

All said and done, he did not go back to his parental house in Darjipara after coming back from England. He has been living in this quaint flat in Ballygunge all alone for the last seventeen years. But everyone in his family understood it—meat and eggs are strictly prohibited in the Roy household. Anupam's mighty uncle somehow managed to introduce fish in the house. It is well known that people who have lived abroad for a good many years cannot have dinner without meat and breakfast without eggs. Anupam also keeps receiving foreigners and VIPs. His home is more like a public space. People keep coming, irrespective of their castes or their timings. This is why his family in Darjipara is tacitly grateful to him, though he is not living with them.

That did not mean that Anupam was selfish. He had been requesting his mother, his brother Nirupam, and his sister-in-law Bithi to come and stay with him. They did not come. Bithi's parental home is in Darjipara and she would not move from there. Niru went for evening addas at Shyambazar crossing. His mother said, 'How can I leave our ancestral house? Here is where our deity Radhamadhav resides.' However, Anupam had bought a two-bedroom flat because he guessed things would go like this.

His mother keeps coming. The number of days she spends here might not even add up to two months. But Anupam tries his best. Everybody says that he is a good son.

Anupam does face minor hitches when his mother visits him. There can be no whisky or beer. On those days, Anupam returns home early and ensures that no meat or eggs enter the house. Anupam follows his responsibilities by being hard on himself and derives great satisfaction by hosting his mother for a day or two. He feels the same when Samir stays at his place and he treats him to a plate of fish and rice.

It would have been nice and comfortable had he accepted the offer of Minu Dastur and Ramsharan Agarwal, but he derived greater spiritual contentment by refusing them. This is the pleasure of sacrifice—no less than the pleasure of self-indulgence.

Samir had his meal and fell asleep on the couch. His legs were sprawled on the table, and his knotted unkempt hair fell towards the left. With his back on the sofa, he slept facing the ceiling. His thin chest was heaving slightly along with his breath, his mouth was slightly open, and peeking through his wildly grown beard were two tiny, white teeth.

Anupam seemed to remember something as he saw those two teeth. Something he seemed to remember, but not quite. Someone he knew well had such a pair of white teeth. Who is it? He felt uncomfortable. Anupam will not accept defeat; it is against his nature. He will not even be defeated by the loss of clandestine memory. A terrible struggle ensued. He applied all his mental power to bring back the lost memory. When he finally managed to remember it, after digging and shovelling the past with great effort, Anupam was really surprised.

A long time ago, a squirrel fell from its broken nest in Thakurbari's garden. Nirupam had picked it up and kept it as a pet. The squirrel had a pair of teeth like this.

Anupam never liked keeping pets. They are vulnerable and dependent, these domesticated animals. They take advantage of human strength and reign on them with the tyranny of the weak. This great vice is not only present in pets but also in women, children, the elderly, and the sick. Anupam does not believe in terrorizing the weak, but he will not be ruled by them. He likes friendships among equals—men with men, power with power. However, you cannot look for a reflection of this thought in his political views. There is no tyranny of the weak in the larger world; that exists in personal spaces only.

Nirupam is just the opposite in such cases. Unlike his brother, he is not a rebel and has been voting for the Congress party, just like his father or uncle used to, without any contemplation. He scarcely notices that the Congress government has moved away from the ideals of the Congress party long ago. He will not see how unruly and tortuous the government has become. On the other hand, he is full of affection for all animals on this planet. He used to bring sickly mongrels, lame kittens, and featherless nestlings in the house. He still does all that. The only difference is that he does it on the sly and says, 'Khokon got them.' Niru has not grown up!

Anupam looked at Samir. His right hand is lying defenceless on the sofa, with his palms open, as if they are asking for alms from somewhere above. His left hand is folded on his lap in a polite gesture. As if he has never had any association with violence.

Anupam knows that Samir's right hand is not so innocent. When his vulnerable fingers unite into a fist, they deftly throw bombs and shoot pipeguns. But now, he is sleeping so peacefully facing the sky, his face overflowing with purity, innocence, and helplessness.

THREE

It is two o'clock sharp. He sat at his desk, arranged paper and carbon on the typewriter, and started planning for the rest of the day. 'Roy's Corner' is ready for Sanjeeb. He just needed to go through it once more. It is the twenty-second. If he could not dispatch the oil report by the twenty-seventh, it would not reach Geneva by the fourth. The conference starts on the fourth. Anupam could not attend it as he had a meeting with the prime minister on that day. The prime minister had called a handful of intellectuals to a discussion, seeking suggestions. Anupam felt that it was more important to be active in his own country than deliver theoretical lectures abroad.

A lot of time had been squandered in the morning. Giving driving lessons to Kamalkali is a waste of time; she will never drive a car. Out of one and a half hours, the last twenty-five minutes were useful. No, he does not have much physical needs—he does not want to pay too much importance to something as trivial as his body. But he is not an ascetic after all. From time to time, the mind needs a holiday, a break from things cerebral. The presence of women is not an indispensable part of Anupam's busy life. Just like there is alcohol or cigarettes, there are women. These are comforting for leisure, good to enjoy sometimes, but one can easily do without them. He does not really have any addiction other than coffee. No amount of alcohol or women, fame or power has been able to intoxicate him. He holds the reins of all the horses; everywhere he has drawn the line. A drunkard does not have any armour; he is naked and vulnerable. His intelligence deserts him. Anupam Roy is not at home in a place where intelligence does not work. Intelligence is power; intelligence is the mark of a man. He would rather spend time with a smart guy than a brainless damsel. In case he really craves for some female company, he finds girls like Kamalkali, Nalini Deshpande, or Promila Rohatgi. They are as light as lozenges. But he does not let them enter inside. Anupam is strong that way. His mind is in his control, be it in the smooth alley of alcohol or the slightly choppy waters around the heart. Those sides are stormy and turbulent, and the brain does not really work in that arena. So, Anupam cautiously avoids matters of the heart. Therefore, his manners are perfect; he attends to his responsibilities wonderfully. Politeness is a chemical amalgam of control and tolerance, and it comes to Anupam naturally. One who possesses intelligence also possesses tolerance. A controlled person knows how to endure things. An intelligent person, thus, is never impolite or drunk—it is not possible for him to commit suicide as a jilted lover.

Since these things were transparent to him, Anupam had no worries. He was free. He did not expect anyone in the world to be as considerate and bright as him. Emotions like anger, frustration, or grudge came from the lack of foresight. Clever people knew that no situation could be the 'worst'; every situation was subject to change.

Anupam knew how to protect himself. Still, he spent some extra time with Kamalkali today. He would not give her so much time from tomorrow.

He decided to go through Sanjeeb's matter first. He quickly ran his eyes through and corrected a few proofing errors and put it into an envelope. Taking it out again and rereading the stuff, he felt extremely satisfied. The piece was hard-hitting and sharp. He put it back and pulled out a file. He pushed up his spectacles to the bridge of his nose, and then, in the whirlpool of the black silk ribbon of his portable Italian typewriter, his surroundings, along with the repeated calls of the hawkers from the road and the incessant twittering of the *shalik* birds on top of his window, he vanished.

He was getting into the car after his meeting. Nilabjo, Lalit, and Sati were with him.

'Your voice is sounding hoarse,' Nilabjo said after taking his seat.

Even Anupam had been thinking about this. His throat actually felt sore. It had been quite a while since he crossed forty. Though there had been some snowfall on his hair, his health was perfect. Apart from minor instances of flu and indigestion once in a while, he did not fall sick. Eyes were the only pair of slightly weak organs in his body. But what was wrong with his throat now?

Anyway, he would not worry much about his body.

'Maybe it is due to excessive sweating. It will be fine.'

'Gargle with salt water when you go home.'

'I am not going home now.'

'You will go home some day, some time, right?'

'Lalit disagrees with you,' Sati chirped from the backseat.

'What does that mean? Do you mean to say that Anupam never goes home?'

Nilabjo laughed, 'I am talking about today's meeting.'

'Lalit says our policy is probably wrong. Our kind of publicity might confuse public opinion at this juncture,' Sati said without joining in the laughter.

Anupam smiled to himself—even Lalit has opinions on policy questions! But he spoke seriously, 'How is it so? Lalit, tell me how your thoughts are flowing. May be, there is something wrong in our perspectives.'

Lalit's face lit up like a thousand-watt bulb. The great Anupam Roy wants to know his thoughts! This is why Anupamda is so popular. Lalit started to explain his ideas with great enthusiasm.

Within bouts of attention and inattention towards Lalit's words, Anupam was thinking that the meeting had continued for an incredibly long time. But it was not seven-thirty yet. He would go straight to Mohan Rao's and drop them somewhere on the way. *Uff*! Lalit speaks a lot of nonsense. He needs to be stopped now.

'Yes, I think there might be something in what you say, Lalit. Though it has to be proved....Isn't it so? We have to sit with it seriously some day. Sati, where are you people going? Nilabjo and I are going towards old Ballygunge.'

'No, Anupamda,' Sati said what Anupam had expected her to say. 'You can drop us near Purno Cinema. We have to go home.'

'Lalit is an interesting chap. His ideas are original,' Nilabjo remarked after Lalit and Sati got off the car.

'You bet,' Anupam thought. 'Forget originality, it is just precociousness.' But aloud he said, 'Yes, his ideas are interesting but not politically mature. You cannot shine in practical politics by being so emotional. He needs to cool down.'

'You will not join practical politics. Otherwise the country would have benefitted from it.'

Anupam grinned.

'Benefit! No, it would be disadvantageous. I am just an academician, not a politician. Political analysis and politics are not the same. Is writing poetry and writing on poetry the same?'

'This is not a good comparison. You are using distorted logic. The two domains are different—one is creative and the other analytical.'

'Same here. You need separate talents for these two.'

'You had the talent. Why not use them?'

'Don't say that. Even the God of Bible can't blame me for that.'

Entering the *krishnachura**-covered alley that led to Mohan Rao's house, Anupam saw a red letter box in the corner of the street and remembered that he had received a letter from Sudha in the morning. Since there was no time to read it, he had left it on his desk.

Samir came at midnight. He brought a kitbag with him and asked Keshto to give him a cup of coffee. He said he was feeling unwell and refused to have dinner. Anupam had just returned from Mohan Rao's party and had gone back to his typewriter. Samir could hear the faint rhythm of the machine. Keshto had already made his bed and he went to sleep. He did not want to disturb Anupam. The kitbag was kept under the bed.

While working on his typewriter, Anupam was informed that after hearing a knock on the door, Keshto had opened the door and Samir came and went to bed. Most probably, he did not have dinner.

But the only thing he did not get to know was about the bag.

Samir woke up Keshto at dawn and asked him to shut the door behind him. Anupam had worked late into the night, so he did not call him. He asked Keshto to request Anupam to keep the kitbag safely in an almirah. The bag has Samir's belongings.

'See you at night, Keshtoda,' Samir said and tiptoed out into the darkness.

---

*A flame-red flower that blooms in large numbers towards the onset of summer.

FOUR

Kamalkali's eyebrows, at that moment, were slightly twisted over her doe-like eyes—the green bindi on her forehead was also creased. She clutched on to the steering like a shipwrecked person, holding on to the broken hull. Young men in Calcutta must be envying the steering—the object which is in possession of Kamalkali's attention. Her entire being was centred on her hands, eyes, and feet.

The other side of her mind was alert, of course—sitting beside her was no one but the Anupam Roy. However, sadly, at that moment, it was more important for her to be attentive towards the roads. Otherwise, it could be dangerous.

This was such a bother. She did not like complexities of any kind. To be honest, she was not enjoying the driving lessons at all. She just liked being with him. To think that Anupam Roy was spending his precious time with her, just with her, was a wonderful feeling.

Suddenly, there was a hue and cry on the road. The car came to a screeching halt. Anupam pushed the handbrakes, and Kamalkali's right foot miraculously transferred itself from the accelerator to the brakes. A child, probably from the refugee colony, came in front of the car. He brushed past death just by a few inches. His mother, with some more infants on her lap, quickly got on to the footpath. She was screaming at him for being careless. The boy's face was masked in fear and tears. His lips were slightly parted, but he was silent. He was holding his torn pants. People on the road, strangely, were shouting at him for being careless. Is Calcutta changing? 'Goodness!' Kamalkali muttered under her breath. 'What a mother! Oh!'

Anupam replied calmly, 'The car is on third gear. It will not start. Neutralize it first. Let's stop here today. Leave it to me. Move.' Kamalkali was relieved. She left the driver's seat and took the one beside. Holding on to the steering, Anupam touched Kali's shoulders lightly and said, 'You have to keep a few things in mind while driving, Kali. First, you must keep your cool. You cannot afford to lose your calm, come what may! Second, assume that every pedestrian, driver, cyclist, everyone, without exception, is insane. The question of their propriety or responsibility does not arise. All responsibilities lie with you. Third, assume that pedestrians do not have eyes or ears. They don't hear you honking and they do not even see the cars coming. You are the only person with eyes. If you keep these things in mind, driving will be easy for you.'

Kamalkali had been out of touch with being offered such serious advices at once. She was looking at Anupam—his dusky, elliptical face with huge eyes glistening like an aura behind the thick lenses. You can't keep looking at them for long. A thin moustache over thin lips. You have to look either at his moustache or at the thick frames of his specs. There is a lock of hair over the lines of his forehead, with sweat sticking to his brows. Kamalkali could not pay attention to what he was saying. She really wanted to push his hair back and wipe his forehead with her scented, lace kerchief. The warmth of his arm on her shoulders was increasing. It had begun to burn her entire body. Who wants to listen to a long lecture on driving? But Kamalkali belongs to the civil world. She did not follow her heart, but uttered brusquely, 'Why will I take responsibility of other people's lives? I will just be careful of my own. That is the most difficult task at hand.'

'Ensuring the safety of others is a part of self-defence, Kali!'

'But people will walk in the middle of the road blindly, dogs will jump in front of my car, cows will sleep on the road, beggars will come by the window …'

'Chhi! You cannot talk about human beings and animals in the same breath, Kali!'

'Come on, are animals not living beings?'

Anupam looked at the greenery outside his car and said, 'There is a difference in the worth of different living beings.'

'Whatever you say, I really like dogs. Not stray dogs, of course, but good, well-bred dogs.'

'But a lot of humans die while trying to save cows and dogs. Do not try to save street dogs. They have good self-defence skills, much more alert than pedestrians.'

Kamalkali thought, 'Now you just mentioned humans and dogs in the same breath and I am wrong if I do the same!' But she did not say anything. There is something intoxicating in Anupam's voice, no matter what he says (the way he is talking about cows and dogs and the dumb and the deaf); everything sounds like words of romance. Kamalkali was being unable to concentrate on his remarks.

'Kali,' Anupam pressed her shoulders gently.

'Hmm.'

'Say something. I gave you an advice. Did you listen? Have you understood?'

'No.'

'So what were you doing all this while?'

'All this while? I did this.'

Kamalkali raised her rebellious chin slightly and looked straight into Anupam's eyes. Her petulant lower lip came forward a little, like an open sweet pea flower. Placing her rosebud fingers, one of them adorned with a huge Tibetan ring, on Anupam's thighs, she gave a sure but gentle pressure. Anupam reciprocated just like an automated machine. His hand released Kamalkali's arms, moved towards the gear, and then switched the direction of the car. The car changed its speed. It kept looking for a place as safe and desolate as God's hands. It was time for another teacher and a different set of lessons.

Eisenhower once commented that Ford's coordination is so weak that he cannot do two things at the same time. For instance, he cannot cross the road and chew a gum at the same time. One can say just the opposite regarding Anupam Roy. He can possibly accomplish hundred different tasks with precision at the same time.

They reached a bustling locality. Anupam pulled Kamalkali's cheeks, removed his hand carefully, and checked her forehead. The green bindi was intact, so it was fine.

Anupam was listening to Kamalkali's chatter while looking at the road. Suddenly, his eyes narrowed after spotting someone. He slowed down the car. Was it Ajitnarayan? A madman was standing right in the middle of the road in dirty and tattered clothes. He was shaking his nestlike head and blabbering something. As he came nearer, Anupam realized that it was not Ajit, but an older man. The man got suddenly excited as the approached him. He spat vehemently on the car. Anupam pulled himself away from the window, his right foot pressing the accelerator hard. Kamalkali shivered, '*Issh*! Dirty! What if he spat on you? Why did you go so close to that madman? Who does something like that? *Ishh* ... '

'I thought he is someone I know.'

'You know a madman?'

'I know a lot of madmen and only one mad woman.'

'Ah ... ' Anupam moved his eyes from Kamalkali's colourful features and looked at his own shirt. He hoped that it was not colourful. He would have to detour via the post office after dropping Kamalkali home. He had lots of important work there. Today, he finished with the Kamalkali episode in forty-five minutes. It was going to be nine o' clock soon.

FIVE

After coming back home, as Anupam was surfing through the newspaper, Keshto came to keep the letters on his desk. The coffee was quite good. He informed that Somshankar Duttaray had telephoned and left a message for Anupam to call back. Anupam shuffled through the bunch of letters. There was a largish envelope from Geneva—copies of papers penned by others had already started to pour in. There was a notice of an upcoming seminar from Sapru House and the latest copy of *South Asia Bulletin*. The fourth letter was important; Professor Okura had sent his comments on one of Anupam's essays. Then there was a receipt of electric bills. And there was a love letter from that Gujarati girl. Oh! These people could drive you nuts. She had been sending four letters every week, written in purple ink and sent in green envelopes. This had been going on non-stop for some time now. Anupam tore off the letters without reading them. A photograph was torn in the process—half of a young woman's smiling face fell off the cleavage of a green envelope and went straight into the litter bin.

A proof set had come. His daily analysis of the Bangladesh War was going to be published in the form of a book. But the government still did not want to bring out his analysis of the Indo-Pak War. It was considered unpublishable due to various reasons. Mujibur Rehman's* dream had come true, but how long would it last? Anupam was quite sceptic about it. The way Indians were ecstatic about Bangladesh made Anupam doubt if the revolution led by people like Samir had any future in India. In such times, one could see the flashes of bloodthirsty people in a nation where people are otherwise 'helpless' and 'starved'. Anupam knew that there was a difference between a rebel and a revolutionary. Just as the way communal riots and national struggle were not the same. Though all clashes had one common result—sons died. There were different values in wars, revolutions, and riots. The methods and issues were different. But there was one common factor—death and loss of lives! Anupam, the son of the Roy family, shivered at this thought. But no, all deaths are not the same. Intelligent people should not think that 'sons die'. All deaths were not the same. Everyone is going to die. It matters how one dies, for what cause, and what the person gets after one's death. Anupam straightened up.

Samir had left a kitbag. What was it? It was locked. A thorn of suspicion pricked Anupam. What could the bag contain?

He would have to call Somshankar Duttaray before starting his work. He is a strange man. Both of them used to take part in debates in Presidency College. That is how long they go back. Last year, they had suddenly bumped into each other at the tennis court in the ABC Club. There is no topic that Somshankar does not discuss. He is a custodian of

---

* Sheikh Mujibur Rehman was a Bengali politician and statesman. He is considered to be the main driving force behind the independence of Bangladesh.

world culture as well as the intelligence branch of Calcutta Police. Anupam got through Somshankar on telephone. The latter apologized for his sudden call and requested Anupam to come for lunch at one o'clock at the ABC Club today. He needed some advice regarding an important matter. Anupam had a class at two in the university. It is ten now. He said that it was not possible for him to reach there at one, but he could go at noon. The appointment was fixed and Somshankar thanked him. What kind of advice would Somshankar need? Was it about his children's admission? What else could he ask Anupam?

There was just one more letter left. A student had requested for a testimonial. Oho! He had not opened Sudha's letter yesterday. This is where he kept it. He looked around but did not find it. He looked again. Nah! Was it in the briefcase? No. Where could the letter go? Anupam starts working with the typewriter whenever he feels jittery. He did that now. He could easily work for an hour or so before going for the lunch. He decided to finish writing the testimonial now. At least one work would be done with.

Sudha had also asked for a testimonial for her job in Hyderabad. Anupam had written and kept it. But Sudha never came to take it. She got the job anyway. It had been two to three months now. Sudha did not irritate him anymore. She had become such a pain that she had to be moved. Anupam was almost 'rude'. He can do anything in a polite and mellow fashion—this is his trademark—but when it came to Sudha, his ability disappeared.

Of course, he was grateful to Kamalkali for this specific reason. Could Sudha have exited from his life so easily if

Kamalkali did not enter? Maybe, she still would. But there were other issues. Sudha is made of a different stuff. She belongs to a different world. Anupam does not know her make or her world. He does not want to know. He does not have the time. No one can have complete knowledge about everything and everyone.

Is Sudha a mystery, an enigma? No, she is very ordinary, though not your run-of-the-mill types. But he does not feel like calling her unusual. If someone does not fall under the standard code of conduct, you cannot label the person as extraordinary. Sudha is on the wild side, thus difficult to comprehend. Anupam knows the ways of the civil world. There, girls are of two types: either normal and domesticated, such as Bithi, Maria, Sati, and the like, or normal and outgoing, such as Kamalkali or Nalini. The other category is abnormal, such as Menaka and Promila. Sudha must be differently abnormal; she is wild.

Anupam just realized that he had been sitting in front of the typewriter for a very long time. He was yet to write anything after 'To whom it may concern'. He suddenly got very embarrassed, looked at his watch, and decided that there was still time to finish writing the testimonial. The tamed, loyal machine took him to the undying world of words.

Keshto, on hearing the typewriter from the kitchen, muttered to himself, 'If he starts working now, when will he take his bath and when will he go for his lunch?'

Anupam put his student's testimonial in the letter box and reached ABC Club for lunch at five minutes past twelve. Between Somshankar's teeth was a German pipe made of polished ivory. Salt-and-pepper hair amidst bald patches, curiously bright eyes behind library-framed glasses, red lips beneath a military moustache almost joining the sideburns, a squarish face, and fair skin on a muscular body—the remarkably good-looking Somshankar Duttaray got up from his seat like a tall tree. Undoubtedly, a tall man like him cannot enter through all doors with ease. After a round of pleasantries, both of them sat at a table.

'Whiskey?'

'No. Gin and lime. It is really hot today.'

'Your voice sounded slightly hoarse over phone. I could not recognize at first.'

'Yes, even I noticed that I am losing voice at times from yesterday.'

'You should take care of it. Your voice is a national treasure ... ha ha ha ha! Did you inhale the vapour of tincture benzene before going to bed? It is very good.'

'I will take some measures today. What's the news on your front? How are you?'

'What news will I have? People like us lead a drab life. By the way, the recent Kurosawa retrospective is a piece of news. How many movies did you watch?'

'I could not go. Was very busy checking papers. Did you watch them all? How many were there?'

'I'd never miss him. Not for my life! Kurosawa is Asia's pride. Of course, we have Satyajit Ray, our own wonder! But Kurosawa's mettle is different. And he also has crudeness and cruelty, something which is not there in Ray's films. Kurosawa is beside the tender and sublime.'

'The Japanese culture has cruelty embedded in its tradition. Indian culture does not.'

'Yes, that is right. But ... '

Somshankar tipped off the pipe on the ashtray and said, 'I am highly impressed with the way Kurosawa handles the theme of cruelty. This time I watched four films, all of which were extraordinary. One of them ends with a scene shown from a distance with purple smoke rising—the entire movie is in black and white, and the use of symbolism in the purple smoke scene is wonderful.'

'But Satyajit Ray has also suddenly brought colours in the last scene of *Gupi Gayen Bagha Bayen*. That is also symbolic.'

'Yes, but Kurosawa's film came before that.'

'Oh. Good.'

The bearer kept Anupam's gin and lime on one side of the table and whisky and soda on the other side. There was a bucket of ice, a pair of silver tongs, and a bowl of nuts between them.

'No matter how hot it is, I prefer whiskey,' Somshankar said while making his drink. 'The soda creates trouble. The colour does not come out properly. I am out to search for the eternal amber. Ha ha ha!' Somshankar's hearty laughter echoed in the room. He pointed at some Chinese sketches of speeding horses and said, 'Have you seen these horses?'

'Of course! My eyes are tired of seeing them.'

Somshankar looked inside his cheroot and said, 'Two things never tire me—whiskey and horses. No, I am not taking about races—there are hardly any races in Kolkata. If you have to bet, you have to go for Derby and Ascot. Of course, there are quite a few good horses in Kolkata. They are world-famous. Mayer, a horse who won the race thrice, was born in Calcutta. Her grandson is with us, at the Calcutta Police. He is a rare beauty. The moment you see him, you realize why horse is called a noble animal.'

'I dislike the use of the word "noble" in the context of animals from my very childhood. The dislike still remains. Only a person with intelligence and conscience can be noble. Right?'

'Ha ha ha! It shows clearly that you are not an animal lover. Another gin and lime?'

The waiter had come back, this time with the menu card. Lunch was usually not served here before one. It was being served at twelve-thirty because of Somshankar's special position.

'Let me order a steak. How would you like it?'

'It is good to order it in medium quantity. The way meat is served in this country, I do not have the courage to have it underdone.'

'Do not worry about that,' Somshankar laughed.

'Order whatever you want. It is merely a ritual. It is going to be "well-done", very well-done.'

A lady started playing the grand piano at the other end of the room.

'The lady has just started taking piano lessons,' Somshankar said in a low tone.

'How did you understand?'

'Her hands are not set. She is playing a pastoral. Can't you recognize? It is a plain tune.'

'It sounds familiar. Of course, I don't understand music. I can't distinguish Beethoven's compositions from Mozart's.'

'Chhi! Don't talk like that. Even a person who knows music can be duped regarding such things. Once I made a fool of myself at Vinu Khandelwal's house in Delhi.'

Somshankar took out some fine tools from his pocket and started cleaning his pipe meticulously. His whisky was almost over.

'How come?'

'It is a funny story. Bearer! Please get one more whiskey and one more gin.'

'Cancel my drink. I have a class at two. I won't have another.'

'Na—take one more drink—will you have beer with steak? Red wine is not good here. It's too heavy and sour.'

'Na, nothing else.'

'Have a glass of gin then.'

The smoking, sizzling pieces of beef arrived on two wooden platters, along with vegetables, roasted potatoes, and mushrooms—sizzler, the most desired dish of modern civilization. Anupam kept contemplating—how much has this dish progressed from the times of the cavemen?

'In Khandelwal's house,' Somshankar put back the pipe-cleaning tools in his pocket, carefully carved out a piece of beef, doused it in French mustard and Worcestershire sauce, and put it in his mouth along with the mushrooms. He kept chewing with his mouth shut. After he was done, he said, 'An instrumental piece was playing. Khandelwal said he will gift a scotch to the person who will be able to identify the musician. I clearly felt it was Bach. So I ... '

'Then?' Anupam asked while mincing the meat silently in his mouth and checking the time on his wristwatch. 'Did you win?'

'I said, "Bach, any bet?" He said, "If it is wrong, then you will pay for the scotch." I agreed in a frenzy. There was a Russian mathematician there. He said smilingly that it was Electronic Bach, created by him and composed in a computer. Bach is a lot of maths, so a mathematician can easily imitate him. You must have noticed that mathematicians are quite often musicians—Einstein, Satyen Bose, and others.'

Anupam's time was getting wasted. Today, he was giving lessons in films, painting, horses, Western classical music, art, and culture. This was the reason why he could never be friends with Somshankar. Somshankar is undoubtedly talented, but way too much. He should have been a professor instead of being in the police. It seemed he was ashamed about choosing this profession.

Anupam said, 'I have no knowledge of or knack for Western classical music. I like low music like Paul Robson, Billy Holliday, Louis Armstrong, or Ella Fitzgerald.'

'*Babah*! Why should they be lowly? They are all prodigies. I respect them. And why only them? I also like contemporary singers like Bob Dylan, Joan Baez, and Pete Seeger. Do you remember Pete Seeger's performance in Park Circus Maidan in 1963?'

'Of course! I still have goosebumps—"we shall overcome"—"keep your eyes on the prize hold on"—unforgettable!'

'You better deposit the kitbag in the police station.'

Did the piece of beef inside Anupam's throat turn into stone? His hands clutched on to the knife and the fork for a second, and then got back to work. He was about to ask, 'Which kitbag?', but knew such questions would be fruitless over here. Anupam groped for words. Words ... have all words deserted him? He carved out another piece of meat and a whole potato in the fork, and shut his mouth for a few minutes. Both of them were completely silent.

Somshankar said again, 'Check if there are incriminating things in the kitbag. Or you will be in trouble.'

Half-eaten delicacies lay on the plate. Anupam laid the knife and fork and took a sip of the gin.

'What happened? Is the meat too hard?' Somshankar looked for a while at Anupam after mouthing the last piece of meat along with a slice of tomato and lettuce. 'Why won't the meat be tough? It is of a very bad quality. There is no quality control in this country. What will you lecture on at two o'clock? Journalism or political affairs?'

Anupam said, 'I can't deposit the kitbag at the police station. They are my students.'

Somshankar broke into a smile and said with affection, 'You have to be practical. Even you are a class enemy to them. Don't forget that. You deposit it yourself. Even if we conduct a search, no case will be lodged today. The problem will be solved.'

Samir's smiling eyes floated before Anupam. He was holding a glass of transparent, cold drink with a fresh, green slice of lime swimming inside. Was Anupam's bespectacled face also bobbing up and down in the same glass? What will you do now, Anupam Roy? The key to his future lies in Samir's kitbag.

Somshankar was muttering something.

'People in this country expect so much from someone like you. You should not get embroiled in such petty issues. It is as bad as playing with fire.'

They can play with fire, but can't you, Anupam?

'I saw your article in *South Asia Bulletin*. It is wonderful. You are a brilliant analyst. But you sound too critical in *New Left Review*—isn't it so? As you can understand, your writing reaches the world. The country's image will be created through writings of you journalists. We badly need your constructive criticism at this critical hour.' How strange! Why would Somshankar Duttaray come and lecture Anupam? What did he know? He was getting so much adulation, alcohol, and meat just because he was an academic—there was no doubt about that. This had been decided by Somshankar himself—a king treating another king. Only an intellectual can preserve another intellectual.

'Please don't take it otherwise, don't mind my saying this. I thought it is best to clear things with you. They are fighting a lost game. They can never win.'

A lost game? Anupam? Can't you win? Recall Badal's face, the tiny pair of Samir's teeth. Remember what you said in the meeting yesterday. Recall what you wrote in the article that you handed over to Sanjeeb. It must be with the compositor now. Anupam, do not deposit the kitbag; keep it in Darjipara. Of course, that place will also be searched. No one but Sudha, only Sudha would have agreed to keep it with her. But Sudha—achcha, how about throwing it into the river or in the Dhakuria lake?

The waiter cleared the plates and kept the menu card on the table. 'Please have truffle pudding,' Somshankar said while going through the menu. Anupam shook his head in disagreement.

'Then have a peach Melba or a chocolate sundae? Banana fritters maybe? Nothing?'

Anupam shook his head again. Somshankar returned the menu and started filling the pipe with tobacco of the Balkan Sobranie variety.

'Coffee?'

'I can have a quick cup of coffee. Black.'

'Two cognacs, two cups of black coffee, demitasse, and a packet of India Kings cigarettes. I ordered everything together since you are in a hurry for the lecture.'

Anupam suddenly found Somshankar's company unbearable. He still needed to have coffee and cognac, and maintain a polite conversation with him. A wave of resentment surged through his body—Anupam, are you so impatient? Somshankar is a friend. Hear his friendly talk, look at his friendly smile. He would not have warned you had he not been a friend. If intellectuals do not protect each other ...

Somshankar was smoking his pipe carefully. An expensive, foreign fragrant spread in the air, ruling the room in a manner befitting him.

Coffee, cigarettes, and cognac arrived. Anupam sipped the drink. There was a burning sensation through his throat to chest. Somshankar was offering him India Kings. He carefully lit the cigarette for Anupam. After discussing the various brands of tobacco, Somshankar was now delivering a lecture on cognac. Three-star, five-star, VSOP, champagne, cognac. Anupam knew all this very well. He has talked about these things himself so many times. Such dialogues do the rounds in all the parties—from one voice to the other—the same amusement—same permissiveness, same joke, same gossip—same brand of pride camouflaged in humility—string of words and sentences. It was getting late. Did he really need to submit the kitbag? Anupam brushed the ash off his cigarette and sat up. His throat felt like a dry pond, as if someone has gripped his voice box. He tried to clear his throat for some time, then said in a hoarse voice, 'Thanks. Good that you informed. Let me see how I can warn this fellow. He will be in trouble if he comes to pick up the bag' (He is supposed to come today, Anupam thought). Somshankar's moustache quivered in an affectionate smile, 'You people need to grow up. You analyse such complex political situations so subtly, and you cannot address such a trivial issue? We can easily arrest the guy who visits you every day, can't we?'

'Then?'

'Arré, we got to know about a lot of dens while stalking him. He is a very careless boy. He did not even get an inkling of our chase. By the way, you write wonderfully, but if you could please change your orientation ... I mean if you could write something more constructive on the national front. It is best not to be too sympathetic towards them—the government has taken a stern attitude on this.'

'Thanks for letting me know. But I have to go now. Bearer, please bill this in my account.'

'Certainly not. Don't be absurd. You are my guest. What's thc harm in being my guest here? We are not hosting you in the "other" guest house. Ha ha ha ha! I asked you to come here so that that does not happen. Ha ha ha ha!'

The hall was almost deserted. Somshankar's spirited laughter crushed the upmarket silence prevailing around.

The half-baked pastoral had stopped—Somshankar's bellow of laughter reverberated like stein gunshots in Anupam's heart.

Anupam somehow managed to escape a bunch of worried students. Some students were still following him. He had suddenly lost voice while delivering his lecture today. All of a sudden. He excused himself and came out of the class. The lecture was left incomplete. He got into the car and refused to talk to his students. 'Where to now?' Anupam thought as he placed his hands on the steering.

Darjipara, he thought. He needed to see a doctor too. Their house physician has a clinic there. He needed to know if he has caught a cold. Where would he go after that?

Can't Anupam go stronger than the law? If the government shows stern attitude, can't Anupam be sterner? No, he can't. After all, he is just a person, an individual. He is not an institution.

The kitbag.

Once he reached Darjipara, Anupam telephoned Keshto and asked him to give the kitbag to Samir when he comes. Samir has to spend the night in some other place as Anupam's mother is coming with him.

He did not speak much, but even that short conversation made his throat pain. He would have to come tomorrow as the doctor was not available now. So he returned home with his mother.

Samir had not come—Anupam got to know as soon as he reached home. The kitbag eyed him like a cat from under the bed. He had hoped that the problem will be solved on its own, that the owner of the kitbag would collect it himself. But this was an illogical hope, an impossible dream. What next? A glass of cognac and whisky would do now. But that was not happening; Ma was here. Anupam prepared himself. He picked up the kitbag and spoke as clearly as possible, 'Keshto, I am going out. Do not open the door if Samir or Badal comes.'

Keshto was in the kitchen. He stepped out to verify what he heard, 'Yes, Dadababu? I should not open the door … ?' Keshto realized that he had heard it right. Anupam saw mangled distrust in one of his eyes and aversion in the other.

Anupam did something which he never did. He spoke intolerantly, though his voice was almost inaudible, 'Do as you are told. Do not open the door for anybody and everybody.'

He went down the stairs, his shoes clamouring impatiently. The car door was slammed. It took a powerful start and moved on recklessly with Samir's kitbag inside. Then the car disappeared down the lanes like a fallen star.

SIX

After coming out of the police station, Anupam went straight to the *Daily News* office. He had to find out about the matter he sent Sanjeeb the last time. It was not typeset yet. He brought back his piece. It had to be edited; the approach had to be altered.

He bumped into Pulak at the newspaper office. He even met Dastur there. Dastur called, 'Come, let's have a session today. Been long since we had one.' Pulak is a proofreader with an English daily and writes short stories for Bangla magazines. Anupam knows that Pulak has made a name for himself. But he has not read Pulak's work; there's no time. He likes Pulak a lot—he is a sincere chap. He excused himself from Dastur and left the office with Pulak. He should get to know what the young people are thinking and writing these days.

He was feeling suffocated. Anupam felt the need for freedom, a breath of fresh air. Green Dragon Restaurant was good in this respect. It has a lawn.

Ah! How Anupam's throat longed for fresh air. The wave of a melody swept over his heart, the tune of *tomar khola hawa, lagiye pale, chino korey kachi, ami dubte raji achi,*[*]

---

[*] Lines from a song by Tagore ('I want to surrender my sail to your unbound wind/breaking all shackles, ready to drown').

but Anupam did not pay attention to the absurd ideas of the song. Who would be ready to drown? Nobody could break all the shackles.

Anupam brushed aside the lyrics, but the song kept whirling inside him like a potter's wheel. He shattered the vessel that was talking within him and broke into a conversation with Pulak, 'So, what are you writing these days? Something new?'

'I have started writing a novel.'

'Excellent. Must be really good.'

'Let's see what luck has planned for me.'

'What luck? If you write something, it will come out well.'

'Not really. My work is of a mechanic. The rest depends on someone else.'

'Are you talking about the readers' choice? You should not leave everything on the readers.'

'If I could give myself up to the custodian of success, there would be no problem. That is what I cannot do.'

The drinks arrived. Anupam is not having ice due to his sore throat today.

The drink tasted bland without ice. A hot cup of coffee must have been a better option. It felt as if someone was clutching his throat from within. Suddenly, there was a slap on Pulak's back.

'What's going on? Whispers, secret rendezvous, huh? Eating out? So you are freeloading these days, Pulak?'

Ah! Anupam helplessly saw that Ramen has made his entry with his typical jokes. Even so early in the evening, he was half-drunk.

'May I know what you were discussing?'

'Pulak's writing.'

'Not exactly. About success and God.'

'Oh! Pulak's god! I thought God Himself. Pulak does not have a single god; he has goddesses. Oops! Sorry!'

Ramen winked and drew a female form in the air.

'Of course not, Ramenda. Please do not crack such jokes.'

'You rascal, you are lecturing too much nowadays. How many proof sets did you check today? Yes? How many hours? Tell me.'

This was below the belt, thought Anupam. Pulak considers himself an artist. He does not like to identify himself as a proofreader. Anupam got even more irritated with Ramen. Anupam hated silly pretexts instead of real logic. Ramen was trying to be clever, as he lacked strength. Anupam added, 'Pulak is busy writing a novel.'

'I see.'

Ramen smiled through his bearded face. 'Thou too Brutu, eighteen chapters in eight pages? Is the latest novel coming out this puja? God bless thy child and thy readers too. God! Forgive them as they do not know what they are doing.'

'Ramenda, do you believe in God?'

Pulak threw an abrupt question.

'No, Sir. I do not believe in any unearthly creature or creator. Got it?' Ramen poured the rest of Pulak's drink down his throat. Without paying heed to his action, Pulak continued, 'Of course, you do. You are an artist, right? Your aethism is all rubbish. You could not create such paintings without believing in God.'

'Why? That man used to write books earlier. Four Vedas, two Bibles—he has written quite a lot. Is he also painting nowadays? Huh?'

'Ramenda, how old are you? Must have crossed forty?'

'Why?' Ramen rescued his tiny pair of nickel-framed specs out of his beard and said, 'Are these looking like reading glasses or the eyes looking like specs?'

'Ramenda, look at yourself now. This is not lack of humility but profuse disrespect towards your own being. Humility and respect are as essential as light and air for an artist, Ramenda.'

'Please stop, dear. Don't deliver lectures. Anupambabu, order three drinks, please?'

Anupam was also irritated. These people were discussing nonsensical things. Instead of coming here with Pulak, he could have gone with Dastur, or even working on the paper from home would have been a better idea. Even the evening breeze refused to blow today. On some days such as this, there was no breeze at all.

'Ramenda, please look at yourself. How can we create something timeless with such a restless mind?'

'High philosophy, huh! Who are you? Maharshi Mahesh Yogi or an imitation of Christ?'

'Do not take it lightly, Ramenda. You should not joke about this. Don't you remember that *shloka* from Gita where it says that a person who is overcome by his/her six inner enemies* insults the God that resides within, and that it is a heinous sin? And the way those sinners are punished.... I can't even visualize. *Ahamkaram, balam, darpam.*'

Ramen might not know this *shloka,* but Anupam remembered the lines very well.

ahankaram balam darpamkamam krodham ca samsritah
mam atma-para-dehesupradvisanto 'bhyasuyakah

tan aham dvisatah kruransamsaresu naradhaman
ksipamy ajasram asubhanasurisv eva yonisu

His father read the Gita aloud every day. How could he forget his father's Bhagavad *path*? But Anupam did not utter the *shloka*s. He did not give a cue about the *shloka* to Pulak. He sat still as before.

* The six inner enemies refer to the six *ripus*, namely, lust or desire, anger, greed, arrogance, attachment, and jealousy.

'No, please. You have made those things up.' Ramenda did not remember anything. He never even knew this. 'Don't nag, please. Listen, even women are better than gods. Do you get it?'

'Women? Better than gods'? Anupam thought. Women are better anyway. At least, when you compare them to God. So real they are. They come when you call them, they react, and they are tactile; a tangible truth. No, women and God cannot be compared.

'Please be serious, Ramenda. Look at yourself closely. Why are you wasting yourself in this manner? There's still time.'

'You swine, you are worse than my wife! I keep asking that woman to get lost, go away to her parents' home, or go and die—but she does not budge an inch. She keeps saying, "Why are you wasting yourself, why are you wasting yourself?"—driving me mad. She does not die, nor does she get away. Can't she elope with someone? She is still juicy....'

'Ramenbabu! What is this?'

Anupam's voice, decently low, did not reveal the tremors of his restlessness or anger at all. His words fell with a sharp metallic thud, like a master pacifying his mad elephant. Everybody fell silent at that moment. The darkness around got thicker; in the trimmed bushes, tiny colourful bulbs kept flickering like fireflies. Somewhere at this odd hour, a bird's shrill cry pierced through the darkness. *Im—po—tent ... Im—po—tent ... Im—po—tent ...*

Anupam ordered for drinks, not three but two, and also asked for the bill.

'I will not have any more. I have to leave early. It would have been nice if I could sit for a little longer, but my mother will be waiting at home.'

His lips spread, as they do when a person smiles; but he did not actually smile, it was practiced politeness. No, he would not like to stay back. He did not like it here. Pulak was used to hearing Ramen's slangs, but Anupam was not. He had come for a relaxed chat, like a human being, to spend the evening in a quiet corner. Was this an occasion to discuss God? At this age? There was a time for everything. In his youth, when Anupam was getting initiated into the discourse of Marxism, he too had to think about God anew. There is no real Marxist in this world who has not thought seriously about God once. You can only reject something when you have thought about it. Even today? No, absolutely not!

Ramen had fallen completely mum. But Pulak was very excited and continued, 'A person who says that he does not want God is either a liar or a saint. I will never accept that humans do not think about God in times of defeat or disasters, or at a moment of fall. Humans, after all, have not reached perfection yet.'

'No, brother, thank you. I am good enough for myself in this lifetime. I do not need your omnipotent God,' Ramen said in a surprisingly calm tone.

Anupam liked this statement of Ramen's, though he found him obnoxious otherwise. He could not but respect self-confidence. Blind faith in God uprooted a person's self-confidence. Belief in God meant dependence, captivity, and subservience. Modernity basically flowed against God.

'Ramenda, if only you could think about it once—'

'Who told you that I have not thought about it?' Ramen banged on the table and suddenly roared. The table shook and the ice cubes clanked against the glasses and laughed, as if it was a joke.

'A boy who has not thought about rejecting his parents' and God's authority when he was sixteen has not grown up at all. He is not an adult. He will sit at home and write poetry like you. Understood? A man who has not thought about women and death at twenty-five has not come of age. These are similar. Listen, brother, I am not a fool. I have rejected him long ago.'

'Right! Absolutely true!' an unfazed Pulak said with doubled enthusiasm. Anupam noticed that his cigarette had burnt and the filter was burning; it was a long streak of ash. 'He would not realize until he scalded his finger,' Anupam thought. He thought of asking Pulak to throw away his cigarette. But Pulak's enthusiasm gripped Anupam with a strange lethargy. He could not get himself to speak.

'Right,' Pulak chirped again. 'But you cannot stop at that rejection. If you are stuck there, it has to be assumed that you have a problem of confined adolescence. The objective of art is to rejuvenate, not to abandon. I am sure you will agree that the purpose of art is not rejection, but resurrection?'

Pulak shrieked mildly upon discovering the burnt cigarette and threw it on the ground. The grass and the soil absorbed the flames without any protest. The very last of the sparks disappeared.

Pooh! What nonsense was being discussed today? The whole evening was wasted. Have all other topics of discussion been exhausted? Death, art, God, and so on—wasn't there anything else to talk about? No important matter? No, no more inertia. Pushing the chair with great force, Anupam stood up. But the lawn did not allow any sound; the knife-like sharpness of the steel chair was easily muffled by the green earth beneath.

Was it past nine? A slimy centipede wriggled through Anupam's flesh, moving under his skin. Did he come? He carefully knocked thrice. Knocked again. Again. Again. The door did not open. Did he leave? Where did he go?

What was on Samir's mind when he left?

SEVEN

Ma asked as he got home, 'Swaraj's wife had called. Were you supposed to visit them?'

Swaraj's wife is Kamalkali. She takes it for granted that somewhere, somehow, they will get to meet daily. They did not meet today.

'Any more letters for me, Keshto?'

'No, Dadababu.'

'May be this letter,' Ma said, holding an envelope. 'It was lying under the bed.' The letter was from Sudha. Sudha's letter. Anupam took it from his mother. He looked at her hands while taking it—pale, thin and dry, full of veins, just like a dried leaf. Was the palm looking like a leaf? Do palms dry up like leaves?

'I am worried about your throat, Anu. I have kept some salt water in the bathroom. Go and gargle with it. That must improve your condition.'

As he gargled, Anupam looked into his mouth's reflection in the mirror. A hole with a set of teeth, strangely animal-like, a fleshy tongue swinging inside, and his nostrils resembling two pipes of darkness. How ugly! Did Kamalkali look like this when she gargled? Anupam looked up at the ceiling.

A lizard. Light-coloured and slithery. Its eyes were as expressionless as glass beads. Its gaze was fixed on an insect. The insect refused to move. Anupam stopped gargling and waved his hands to shoo it away. The insect still would not budge. He rolled a piece of paper and hurled at it. The lizard moved almost immediately. 'Reptiles,' Anupam murmured. The insect had not stirred. Anupam lowered his face and filled his mouth with water; the moment he looked up, he saw the insect struggling to free itself from the lizard's mouth. *Dhush*! Serves it right. This is what happens to stupid people. He tried to warn the insect, but it did not listen. What would Anupam do?

Gargling did not clear Anupam's throat. When he wanted to say 'Ma', a complex sound like 'mmhh' came out. His mother said, 'Anu, call up the doctor and see him tomorrow. I am not getting a good feeling about it. This does not seem all right.'

Anupam took an appointment. He would visit their house physician Dr Chatterjee at eight the next day.

Keshto did not say anything during dinner.

Anupam did not ask anything either.

Did someone come?

Nobody came?

Keshto served food like a puppet. He was not his usual chatterbox self. Anupam also ate silently. His mother was sitting in front of him. Right then, he heard knocks on the door.

Anupam's hand froze inside the bowl of fish. Keshto was coming with a container of rice. He too became still.

There was another knock. Anupam kept staring at his plate, aware of Keshto's eyes like a beam of laser, scanning his forehead, penetrating deep into his flesh and bones and creating a ruckus in his brains.

One more knock now. It was getting sharper. It seemed like there were gunshots and cannons exploding in his head. Anupam felt like putting his almost static hands up in the air and screaming, 'Keshto, do not look at me like that. I cannot take it anymore. I surrender.'

Ma said, 'Why have you stopped eating? Keshto, serve him the rice.' His mother could not hear the knocks—Ma, can't you hear? You are old and hard of hearing. That's why you are spared. Can't you even hear me shrieking? Can't you see Keshto pointing a bayonet at me? Ma? You were never able to hear my cries since childhood or see my wounds. All my gore and wounds have remained invisible to you. There were no more knocks. Just like a film scene which was deliberately paused with a button and then played, Keshto suddenly moved. He got the plate of rice to the table. Anupam waved his hand in disapproval. No more rice for him.

Ma said, 'What happened to you, Keshto? Why did you suddenly stop while walking up to the table?'

Anupam wanted to say, 'Ma, keep quiet.'

Keshto said, 'I felt as if something was burning in the oven....'

Right at that time, the doorbell rang unmistakably. There was no knock this time. Keshto looked straight at Anupam. Anupam's eyes were fixed on the door. Ma said, 'Keshto, please open the door. God knows who has come so late at night.'

Anupam got up from the chair noisily and said, 'Leave it, let me see.'

'Come, Samir. Sleep on my bed. I will watch over you through the night. I will be awake. I have surrendered your kitbag at the police station. But there will be no more mistakes. Come, brother. Jesus had predicted, "Before the cock crows thou shalt deny me thrice"; I will falsify this. It will not be repeated. I will not say like Peter, "I know this man not." I always try to think coolly, considering the pros and cons. That's why I made this mistake. I surrender kitbags when I get time to ponder. Do not give me time to think.'

There was a young inspector at their door. He greeted upon opening the door, 'Sorry to disturb you. We have a search warrant.' His hands, with the warrant, came towards Anupam's like a friend's.

'Come in,' Anupam turned sidewards and let them enter his apartment. The inspector, along with three other men in their clanking boots, entered the apartment.

Ma got surprised at the suddenness of events. She stood up and pulled the saree over her head. Keshto's lips opened in the shape of the letter 'o'. Anupam said, 'Keshto, please be with them. Ma, you go to your room. There is nothing to worry. It is just a routine check. Nothing to worry about.' Anupam smiled, consoled his mother as he thought appropriate, and moved to the other room in light steps.

EIGHT

He woke up with a call from an unknown person the next morning; it came from a wrong number. It was already late. Anupam would sit at the typewriter after going through the letters and newspapers quickly. He would have to rewrite the piece that he got from the newspaper's office yesterday. He was making these plans while brushing his teeth. Then he felt like testing his voice. 'Keshto,' his voice sounded hoarse and distorted. Like a flash of lightning, he remembered that he had an appointment with the doctor at eight! But it was already time. He forgot to check his diary in the morning. Strange!

The doctor was still there. He looked at Anupam's tongue and checked his tonsils. 'Nothing much. I do not see any infection. You neither have a cold. This must be due to tension. Sometimes one loses one's voice due to work pressure. Are you sleeping well? You will be fine if you take rest and gargle properly.' He penned down the name of a tranquilizer on the prescription.

Relieved, Anupam stepped out of the clinic and wondered where to go. Kamalkali had telephoned once. Should he call back? He tore off the prescription. He had ample control on his mind, intellect, and emotions; he did not need a medicine to soothe his nerves. A man who did not have this much control over his mind was not a human.

It was as if his car stopped near Kamalkali's house on its own. Anupam rang the bell. The liveried bearer from Garwal greeted him and escorted him to the drawing room. The room was as cool as a tightly closed jewellery box. Even then, the fan was on. Just when Anupam was about to sink into the plush sofa, Kamalkali's tiny Pekinese dog came from nowhere and started rolling at Anupam's feet. A startled Anupam kicked her unintentionally. It was a reflex action. But this God's creature was not so innocent; she raised shrill cries and brought the house down. This is why Anupam did not like pets at home.

But it is not nice to kick a creature. Anger is a beastly emotion; hatred is a raw natural force. Civilization thrives on self-control—its principal weapon as well as armour. There is no opposition in life that you cannot overcome with the help of self-control.

Anupam suddenly wondered why he was constantly thinking about weapons, victory–defeat, attack, and self-preservation. Did civilization mean struggle and war? Or did it mean peace?

'Yes,' thought Anupam, 'survival of the fittest means war. One who does not have self-control is not fit; he/she is not an evolved human being.'

But the dog. Suddenly. Why? Automatically! His foot. The tiny creature. For no reason. Why?

What has happened to him since yesterday? Is something slipping off his hands?

Anupam carefully picked up the album of Renaissance art from the shining black glass of the coffee table. His eyes caught a painting of young Sebastian—the saint's body pierced with arrows.

Last night....Where is Samir?

Kamalkali had rushed out from her bath. Draping the bathrobe over her wet hair and body, she exclaimed, 'My baby! What's wrong, darling? Why are you crying?'

Her darling had stopped whining by then. She was sniffing in search of cold enmity about the room. Her tiny legs jumped on her mistress' lap and burst into affection. Kamalkali lifted her up and placed a sonorous kiss on her ever-cold nose. That sound abruptly hit Anupam's sensory chords and a fine echo spread through the nerve roots all over his body.

Having wasted a kiss, Kali bursted out in a wholehearted surprise, 'You? How nice! Ram Singh did not tell me. I was in the shower. Ram Singh! How strange! Ram Singh ... '

Her body was fragrant with lavish imported soaps—expensive aroma of foreign soap coming from her body, drops of fragrant water from her hair falling on the Kashmere carpet, the wet hair adorning her makeup-less face, with her cheeks and her forehead in a frame. Droplets on her eyelashes were shining like mica. Kamalkali was looking embarrassed, innocent, and vulnerable. Her bathrobe was light blue and, peaking from her sandals, the string of tiny toenails twinkled like silver.

'What a pleasant surprise!' Kali remarked.

There was no covering or shield beneath that blue robe—just bare Kamalkali beneath it.

Anupam had an intense urge to remove the covering and strongly inhale the imported soap's fragrance with all his senses. He sprang up to his feet like a machine and spread his eager arms wide towards Kali. As soon as he saw a hint of surprise reflected in Kamalkali's eyes, Anupam came back to reality. Meanwhile, the bearer had come to the door upon hearing Kali's call.

Putting on a broad smile, Anupam with his open arms, confidently walked up to Kamalkali.

'Give, let me hold your darling in my lap. She is so tiny, I was about to stamp on her today.'

A gladdening smile lit up Kali's confused eyes at once. With great relief, she transferred her 'darling' to his lap. 'Oh, really? That's why you were crying? Whiny girl! You keep hovering around people's feet!'

She looked at the bearer and asked Anupam, 'What will you have? I will quickly change and come. Cold coffee? Kona coffee? Hot chocolate? Coke? What about some cold beer? What is good?'

'Good?' Anupam wore that special smile which disarms not only women, but everybody, women and men, alike.

'Beer is the best, but I will not have beer in the morning. Give me coffee, black.'

Though he spoke very little, his throat was hurting. The moment he put 'darling' down, she scurried towards her mistress.

'I will be back in a moment. Ram Singh, make Kona black coffee. And a coke for me....What happened to your voice today? *Ishh* ... it sounds strange....'

The book on Renaissance art lay open on the table, its heavy pages trembling gently in the air.

The dog, the bearer, and the mistress—everyone had left now. The empty room echoed the muffled sigh of the air conditioner.

With shaky hands, he went for the book again.

This time, the book opened to a print of Da Vinci's *La Belle Ferronière*. The young lass from Lombardy with a tiara adorning her forehead. Her pursed lips were gentle, but had a hint of stubbornness—there was pride concealed in her straight, clear gaze. Strange! Those adamant lips and such bold, upright glance were very familiar to him. Did she resemble a girl in some other painting? A lot of Da Vinci's paintings were based on the same model. Which picture? Which one? He could not recall now. How could Anupam remember when he had been so restless for the past two days? Where was his concentration? Which painting did the face of this girl resemble? He could not recall.

The air-cooled moments were passing by, companionless. Waiting.

Neither the coffee nor Kamalkali was ready. What was he waiting for?

Anupam suddenly wondered—why had he come here? What did he want from Kamalkali? Being childless, Kamalkali's ample time and entire enthusiasm was focused on climbing the societal ladder. What did Anupam expect from this destitute woman? Why was he here today? In this way? What did he want?

Fragrant and exquisitely dressed, Kamalkali entered with her dog in her lap. She enhanced the beauty of the room as soon as she entered, like a bunch of freshly cut flowers just placed on the table. With the fresh coffee giving out a hint of good smell, good taste, and a little steam, Ram Singh had also come along.

What did Anupam expect here?

A little bit of warmth?

A moment of bliss?

What kind of momentary bliss are you looking for in this suffocating coldness, Anupam?

He did not sit there for long and left as soon as he had finished his coffee. First, his nerves were irritated on seeing a dog being showered with so much attention. Second, who knew that producing sound from your throat would be such a daunting task?

Neither their words nor the touch picked up speed today. His throat was not doing well. Was it just his throat?

Upon returning home, Anupam went to his dearest resort—his desk. He uncovered the typewriter. Some papers fell out as he tried to set them on the machine.

A sealed, brown envelope. His mother had handed it to him yesterday. She had picked it up from the floor. Sudha's letter. He could connect the loose ends of his memory in a lightning speed—now he knew who the girl in *La Belle Ferronière,* with her faint smile and a pair of stubborn, proud eyes, resembled. He now knew why she looked so familiar.

His hands froze for a moment while opening the letter. He kept it back in the drawer without opening it.

Then the typewriter started playing its strange notes, the instrumental music of string letters.

NINE

Ma was sitting in her favourite armchair in the corner of the room. Even though he had his back towards her, Anupam could sense a pair of calm and affectionate eyes looking at him. Ma does not speak much. She speaks even less when she visits her son, lest his work is disturbed. She sits quietly with a Bengali book or her sewing kit. Sometimes, her hands remains hidden beneath the *anchal* of her saree, busy with her prayer beads. At times, she says a word or two like, 'Anu, have you not trimmed your toe nails for a long time?', or 'Your room needs to be dusted all over.' She seldom brings up issues relating to the servants or neighbourly gossip. She was now silently watching her son working. Anupam was trying to check the piece he wrote for the upcoming issue of 'Roy's Corner'.

'Ma, you want to tell me something?' he asked her.

'Your voice. It is not sounding well at all, my dear. Did you meet the doctor this morning? What did he say?'

'He said that nothing is wrong. I have not been able to sleep well in a while. It's nothing. I will be fine.'

'Medicines?'

'He did not prescribe any.'

'Good. God's grace, Madhusudan has been kind.'

Tick-tock, tick-tock—jumped up the types, the hooded snake, and filled up page after page. Keshto came with Anupam's lunch and was returned three times, Ma came and stood silently twice, even the radio news broadcasted in dictation speed was long over. Keshto asked, 'Dadababu, should I eat now?' The write-up was not coming through. No, it was just not happening. This week's 'Roy's Corner' was not getting delivered normally. Anupam was adamant now. Not happening. 'Constructive criticism' refused to come out of his pen, yet you guys will guide the people of this country; your write-ups will be the guidelines to shape the nation's reaction, right? A glass of beer would do now. Whiskey would be even better. But, no, his mother was there. The war went on. The struggle for constructive criticism continued. Ma came again. She rested her hand at the back of the chair and said, 'Anu, it is three. Leave your writing. You better take a break for lunch and lie down for a while. Doctor has advised you to rest. Even I am an old woman. How long will you keep me waiting?'

Anupam was startled. What was wrong with him? He was messing up at every step. He was late for the doctor's appointment in the morning. Then suddenly, the dog at Kamalkali's house. After that, he did something worse—stretching out his arms towards her—what a shame! Although Kamalkali did not fathom his gestures, Anupam himself had no doubt about his intention or the origin of his desire. One more blunder now. He knew that Ma would not eat unless her son ate. That is why he did not delay his meals when his mother was here. On those days, he returned on time for both lunch and dinner. He was at home today. How could he still forget that Ma had been waiting for him? His eyebrows twisted and his face showed that he was disgusted with himself. Anupam got up from his chair.

'Please do not be angry with me,' his mother said while serving him rice. 'You will fall sick if you do not eat now—today is my *ekadashi*[*], I am fasting.'

Anupam looked up at his mother. Pale and thin from fasting, his mother's smile was covered with the shame of a mischievous, young girl.

Ma sat silently on a cane stool and watched her son as he ate. By nature, she did not talk much. 'I will not die in peace till I see you married'—she used to say this from time to time when Anupam sat down to eat. When Anupam's aunt eloped with Arobindo Bhaduri from Dunlop, his uncle took an overdose of sleeping pills. By this, his uncle gave the ultimate verdict even when the divorce case was yet to be closed. Anupam has been let off after that incident; his mother does not ask him to marry any more.

This bizarre modern world had begun to shake up the pillars of Ma's traditional Vaishnava universe, which was restricted to the Darjipara household. A person of few words, Ma spoke even lesser now. Protul was her brother's name. She has never uttered the word ever since.

---

[*] The eleventh lunar day (*tithi*) of each of the two lunar phases which occur in a Hindu calendar month. It is considered a spiritual day in Hinduism and is usually observed by keeping fast.

Ma, you were destined to encounter a lot of pain in life.

Anupam tried to speak in his hoarse voice, 'Has Bishnupriya sent any letters?'

'Yes, it came last Monday. She has sent her daughter's photograph.' Anupam looked at his mother. Gazing down, Ma looked unmindful. Ma, your days have changed, Anupam thought. Bishnupriya, the younger daughter of Darjipara's Roy family now lived as Priya Openheimer in Texas. She teaches a course on Indian civilization there. She sends coloured postcards every week, and also photographs of her blue-eyed daughter. Her daughter has been named Belarani. Anupam's mother's name. Her husband said that it is customary in their country to lovingly name daughters after their grandmother. Her mother, Anupam's jethima*, was called Khemodashundori; but that name would not work. Therefore, they settled with Belarani.

Ma used to imagine her niece and her husband so easily calling out her name throughout the day, 'Bela, Bela.' She felt embarrassed thinking about it. Teary-eyed, she shared her concern with her daughter-in-law Bithi, Anupam's brother's wife, one day. Bithi found it so funny that she laughed it away. Did nobody understand each other's despair in this world? No one could comprehend where your sorrows or joys were coming from. 'Ma, here you are, sitting in front of me, taking care of your child's nutrition routinely. But have you been conscious of my mental nourishment, Ma? I have a body, but a part of me is beyond that body. Did you ever think about that person's well-being or health?

---

* Aunt, father's brother's wife.

You women! You just take care of the external frame. Can someone practice non-violence only by avoiding meat and eggs? Forget meat and eggs, Jethima does not even have fish. The atom bomb at the tip of her tongue has blown up my childhood. But it has not affected you at all. What are you made of, Ma? And you have tears in your eyes thinking that your niece and nephew-in-law are calling you by your name? What bizarre matter is your soul made of?'

'Have one more piece of fish.'

'No, Ma. It's already very late….' (I should not eat any more.)

'Your voice is still terrible. Do not talk....Do you have a lecture tomorrow?'

'Yes, Ma….' (I am thinking what to do.)

'Don't go. Let your throat rest. Can't you take the day off?'

'Yes, that can be done.' (Do I need to take leave already?)

'Do that. Consult an ENT for your throat.'

'Let's wait for a few more days.'

'What did you say? I could not understand a word.'

'I said, let's wait for a few more days.'

'Stop, stop. Don't strain your voice. Your throat is in a very bad condition.'

TEN

After finishing his lunch, Anupam took his position in the battlefield in front of his typewriter. During his meal, he realized that his voice had become worse. It was hurting to say even normal things like 'no more rice', 'some more please', etc. He was getting tired very easily. After speaking just half the sentence, the rest was lost in silence. He decided to take an appointment with Dr Banerjee. This must be an ENT problem, not a nerve issue. Nowadays, doctors categorized diseases as either nervous problems or allergies in order to avoid the trouble of diagnosing. Otherwise, there was the term psychosomatic; that worked a lot. Doctors could classify his throat problem as any of the three. Or the effects of weather change. Or viral infection. Anupam smiled as he thought of these possibilities; everything could be categorized. But he must to go to a specialist now. The ailment had to be treated. He needed his voice back.

The wastepaper basket was stuffed with rejected papers. Anupam waged a war at his desk again. A few phone calls came and some visitors poured in for varied purposes. But not much time was wasted. No one could waste Anupam's time. He could cut his calls short when he wanted. He never let the caller blabber on forever; he said an 'achcha' in a firm, humble, but decisive tone, and put a polite end to the conversation. He had always known the art of turning people away without being rude. That did not mean that Anupam liked to reject; rather he liked fulfilling people's wishes.

The bell rang. Keshto opened the door and came to call Anupam, 'Dadababu.'

'....?'

'Two ladies have come.'

Anupam pushed his chair back and got up.

The two ladies were flipping through a copy of the *Frontier* magazine.

After a round of greetings, they said that they were from the All Bengal Women's League, 'Lady Romola Mitra has sent us.'

No matter how busy he is, Anupam welcomes his guests with a broad and warm smile. He takes good care of his guests, because he knows how to get rid of them. Gently and gracefully, he seizes his own precious time.

Anupam knows a few tricks to send his guests away. After his work is done, he leaves his seat and says 'accha' with emphasis and finality. He does this with utter humility. For people who come to chat and do not stop, Anupam yawns at first and then acts unmindful. He pretends not to hear as the third step. Finally, he stops responding to his guests' words. If all of these fails, he says 'achcha' again. These are his weapons of self-defence.

The representatives of the women's league returned with despair. They were followed by boys from the debating club of St. Xavier's College. Sanjeeb wanted to collect the revised piece today, but Anupam had asked for an extension till the following afternoon. It was just not coming out well. Who knew that writing constructive criticism was such a difficult job! Nilabjo, too, had called; they arranged for a meeting regarding the magazine at Sougata Chaudhury's place. It would be held an hour before the party. He would bump into Lalit and Sati and get into debates again—the idea of talking was stressful to Anupam today. He would not attend the party either. He first needed to complete the two pieces.

'Keshto, a cup of coffee, please.'

Ma came in with a cup of black coffee.

'I sent Keshto to the market, Anu.'

'Even then, why did you take the trouble?'

'What's wrong with it? Not that I do not know how to mix coffee powder in warm water.'

'Not that,' Anupam said as he sipped into the coffee. 'The coffee is very good.'

Ma smiled happily on hearing this. Then she said, 'I am worried about your throat. Please see a doctor tomorrow.'

'Let me see. I will try. Don't worry, Ma.'

As much as he tried, Anupam felt that it was a curse to be a person of good repute. You would have to preserve your reputation. Good reputation came with the burden of maintaining it. The wheel of fame keeps turning. If you want to remain on the top, you would have to toil every moment. Anupam did not abhor hard work, but this writing was not shaping up at all. Even with numerous readings, his old piece seemed alright to him.

His book on India–China conflict was selling better than Neville Maxwell's.* His fancy analysis of the Vietnam War, *The Twentieth Brumaire*, was also on the bestseller list. It was a fantastical theoretical work. Anupam wrote what Marx would have said regarding the Vietnam War if he were alive. It was out in paperback edition in foreign countries and had become extremely popular. His sixth book was about the survival of the Communist Party in the United States during the McCarthy period—a valuable, detailed, leftist analysis. The United States Information Service (USIS) had started favouring him a lot after the publication of this book. However, Anupam did not attend cocktail parties hosted by either leftist or rightist organizations, though he was invited to all of these. Like it was on Marx's 150th birth anniversary—both the parties celebrated the event, but, of course, differently. Anupam had spoken in both the events. He found nothing wrong in it. The topic of his lecture was 'Marx and the Modern World View'. But Sudha did not spare him. Sudha never spared him. She was hardly humble. In spite of being Anupam's research student, her audacity knew no limits. A poor girl from a refugee colony, it took her immense, solitary struggle to stand on her own feet, that too quite late. It was strange

---

* Neville Maxwell (born in London in 1926) is a retired British journalist and scholar. He wrote *India's China War* in 1970.

that she had neither greed nor grudge in her life. Sudha was a strange person, an enigma.

It was a matter of one single evening, a moonlight picnic organized by the department. Just once ... and nothing much ... but that was enough for Sudha to ... that trivial incident.

Anupam truly felt relieved after Sudha vanished from the scene herself.

His coffee went cold; he had drunk half a cup only. He was unable to proceed further with the article. How could he himself reduce the sharpness of his own writing? It was like decapitating it. He was struggling for something as petty as a newspaper article throughout the day. A dilemma over such a small matter!

'Dilemma? There are so many dilemmas in your life. You go through so many conflicts, so much pain!' Sudha's voice spoke silently inside Anupam.

'See, Sudha, when I was young, I did not get a chance to think about what I will be when I grow up. No one ever asked me, so I never thought about it. But I knew that I couldn't be too many things at once, like the keeper of Hiroo, the elephant and Hiroo—or, Anupam Roy and the senior clerk at the Writer's Building*—this much I knew. Sudha, I have become what I am now, without much effort. But now I am forced to put so much effort just to remain what I am.'

---

* The Writers' Building is the Secretariat Building of the state government in West Bengal.

'Dadababu, did you not switch on the light?'

Anupam was startled. Keshto put it on.

'How long are you going to write? Why don't you go out for a short break? Let me get some tea?'

Keshto's eyes looked gentle; they did not pierce him like bayonets today. But this softness stung Anupam more. He sounded harsh, 'Cannot get up without finishing this. It is important. Coffee, black.'

The telephone rang again at eight-thirty in the evening. Anupam felt relieved. Must be Kamalkali. He would go out for a while. It was becoming unbearable. Spending so much time on a trivial article ...

'Hello, Anupam? Somshankar this side.'

'....!'

'Thank you for giving up the kitbag. You know what papers that bag contained? Plus, it had two pipeguns, cartridges, and a notebook. The notebook was a great help. I thought you would like to know.'

'....'

'What happened? Hello, hello?'

'Yes.'

'Is your telephone out of order?'

'No.'

'Can't hear.'

'Samir ... '

'What are you saying?'

'Samir ... '

'Samir? Oh, that boy? He is under arrest now. It was imperative to arrest him after we found the notebook in his bag—for collecting further details.

'Oh ... '

'Not to worry, not to worry. He will be kept alive.'

'....'

'Whatever. Thank you for acting immediately.'

'Should I not thank you?'

'Of course, not. It is just a friendly deed. And I know that it had nothing to do with your own politics—it was merely an act of kindness on your part, obviously. Isn't it?'

'....!'

'A—chcha.'

Somshankar kept down the receiver first and broke Anupam's monopoly of saying a final and polite 'achcha'.

'Ma....?' Anupam croaked dreadfully. 'I will be back soon. Please do not wait for me. Have your dinner.'

The typewriter, with the paper and carbon on its chest, was left bare on the desk. Anupam took his car keys with him. No, not Kamalkali. Nor Nilabjo's party. He wanted to go to

Promila Rohatgi's flat at Southern Avenue. She kept good-quality scotch.

Jesus had said, 'I tell thee, Peter, the cock shall not crow this day, before that thou shalt thrice deny that thou knowest me.'

ELEVEN

Anupam wished to detour via the lake. It felt nice to drive through the lakeside at night.

The reddish moon looked like a huge copper bowl for keeping flowers. His ancestral home in Darjipara had plenty of puja vessels*. One of them now adorned his drawing room as a table. The vessel sheltered a crystal turtle, made in Czechoslovakia. The turtle's body, an ashtray, was a repository of ashes from India and abroad, burnt pieces of matchsticks, and leftover tobacco.

Blowing hard through the window of his moving car, the wind was ear-shattering. The moon, that copper bowl, would now be engulfed by a bunch of black flowers. The pretty visage of the night would be unhappy soon.

The road floated like an ancient boat between the two moonlit lakes. Anupam recalled the scenes painted on Egyptian urns. Trees on both sides of the roads were like slaves rowing the boat. The ruffling of the leaves was like sighs. His car was the throne in the boat. Everything seemed like a very familiar memory—*déjà vu*. When did

---

* Sacred vessels used for offering food to God.

he feel like this before? Was it a long time ago? He lived so close to the lake, but he no longer had the leisure to come and sit by it. But when he was a young member of the Roy Mansion in Darjipara, he used to come this far so often, taking bus no. 2 from Presidency College. Just to sit beside the lake. He spent hours with Lala, Pankaj, and Somnath here.

How old was he then? As old as Samir and Badal.

Lala, Pankaj, Somnath. Where is the triumvirate now? Along with Anupam, they were the four musketeers.

This used to be a safe area for boys from North Calcutta; here, there were fewer chances of bumping into relatives. Not only because they smoked, but Somnath also had a girlfriend back then. Yes, Somnath was the only one to have an affair in their group of four. Manisha lived near Sealdah and went to Brahmo Girls' School. She came to meet her lover near this lake. Pankaj, Anu, and Lala would roam about the lake and practice smoking. Sometimes, the three of them would put their heads together and nervously thumb through the pages of an English book without a cover. Lala used to source such books from Free School Street. Their hearts beat faster than Somnath's that time; their senses were perhaps edgier than his, as they felt guilty and constantly heard the imaginary footsteps of elders coming to spot them.

It was decided that Somnath and Manisha would elope to Bombay after Somnath's exam. Lala's family had a business in Bombay, so he said that he will arrange a job for Somnath there. But Manisha's father deliberately took a transfer to Patna and left with his family. Somnath mourned. He did not shave for a few days and listened to songs of K.L. Saigal. Then he took his BSc exam. Things got sorted when he faced the exam pressure. 'Somnath, do you remember Manisha? All of us were supposed to keep beards that time. Your affair was the first one among us.' Lala, being from Rajasthan, had a wife and a child by then. But a love affair was different. Somnath is currently working somewhere in Texas. It is heard that he is living an affluent and happy life with his American wife. Anupam can meet Lala anytime he wants, but does not feel up to it. Where is the time? Lala runs his shop at Barabazar. He resembles a ripe mango nowadays.

Lala's far-sighted father got his son married before he appeared for his matriculate examination. So, when his car stopped at Presidency College's portico, with the uniformed chauffeur opening the car door for him, Lala used to come out with his son. He went inside the college premises and his son waved him goodbye and ran to Hindu School, which was adjacent to their college. Anupam met Lala last year at his son's wedding. But Pankaj could not come that day.

Pankaj works as a chartered accountant in Durgapur. Anupam went to Durgapur to attend a meeting few days back. Pankaj came to meet him there. A tired-looking man with grey hair, he looked old and had also developed a slight hump. Pankaj used to be the tennis blue and cricket blue in his college days. His wife has been paralysed since the delivery of their first child. The child died a few days after birth. Pankaj's days and nights are spent in looking after his sick wife and going through the daily grind at work. He kept talking about his miseries and failures for so long that Anupam, after being considerably affected by his sorrows for an appropriate amount of time, turned his wrist and shot a glance at his watch. Then he yawned and looked actively, visibly unmindful. Pankaj left his seat and said, 'Anu, I will go now. You are a busy man. I wasted your precious time. Actually, you people have gone far ahead. We are still stuck in those old days. In this small town, we have no sense of time or propriety. The fact that you recognized me is good enough. I should not have stayed on after the exchange of greetings. What say?'

The thin, old-looking man left, leaving someone as smart, sharp, and eloquent as Anupam speechless. He slowly walked out, looking a little older.

Anupam was suddenly feeling hot. It was cool though; the air smelt of dust. He stopped his car and slipped out. The pale full moon smiled daintily across the large, white sky. Across the sky, in the anaemic full-moon light, the dainty moonlike face still floated. On the other hand, wave after wave of black clouds kept dancing. The dark clouds were playing all around the fair forehead of the moon like wisps of hair. They were soon going to cast a shadow over all the light.

Vastness! Leisure! Myriad stars! The marvel of the infinite, unfazed, insurmountable, star-studded universe and the omnipresent moonlight was suddenly suffocating Anupam. Today's full moon was conspiring to drown him—it was showering light like liquid mercury—a hundred times more of the heavy liquid, metal-like moonlight than what the fragile, little vessel of the earth could hold. Just as some infants die under the pressure of their sleeping mothers' breasts, Anupam tried to save himself from the enormous pressure of the indifferent nature. Just like a drowning man tries to stay afloat by putting his nose above the water, Anupam turned his face up towards limitlessness—there the sky was, again. Again, the call of the infinite stars. Each of them spoke of a nameless world and announced its own identity through a distance of light years. One could not keep staring at such proud magnificence for long.

His eyes turned to the earth. The grass beneath his feet was moonlit white. He suddenly recalled the touch of Kamalkali's armpits; removing his sandals, he spread out his feet to feel the tender grass. Wet, hairy, damp soil grass. He placed his warm feet on the grass, but the soil did not seem to be excited.

Anupam suddenly spotted an ugly dwarf grovelling on the ground like a centipede. Who was this dark, malicious, short creature? When did it come? From where? His heels were tied to Anupam's heels. He could not disentangle himself by pulling and kicking the creature. Blood rose in his veins and surged up to his ears, eyes, and face. Anupam looked closely at the solid darkness and found that he was chained to that vermin-like shadowy creature.

He looked around for help. As if he was in his childhood, lost in a fair, not sure about his identity, he sought shelter. He was the only misfit in this deeply synchronized universe. What a pity! How trivial!

A storm came. The cold, petrified air, heavy with dust, struck Anupam's face like a whip. He instantly came back to his senses and found his car waiting for him like a loyal pet. It was ready for its master. He almost rushed inside its womb. It seemed as if this little shelter had saved his life. It felt like this was all pre-planned or something which took place in the past—like ghoulish dreams that are repeated night after night—as if everything was rehearsed. This feeling was called *déjà vu* in French, something that he had seen before. What was it called in Bengali? Nothing? No, there was a Bengali name for this feeling. Anupam had goosebumps as he recalled that word. No ... this had to stop. He had to go now. This feeling needed to be harnessed. He had been very lenient with his not-so-good imagination tonight.

Is such a feeling known as *purba janmo* or past life in Bengali? Memories of the past life?

Anupam started his car. In spite of the storm and of the dimmed moonlight, the lake was still crowded with couples. Suddenly, he was taken aback. Did the boy's gait and his dishevelled hair not look very familiar? No, it was a mistake. Wrapping his arms around a girl's shoulders, this boy walked on against the storm. Could not be him.

But he will be kept alive; he will not be released easily. A lot of information needed to be drawn out from him.

He will not be freed easily Anupam Roy will be kept alive.

Anupam felt that the darkness had turned deeper. The lakeside was getting deserted. He looked for the moon; it had disappeared. But there were two moons a while back: one in the sky and another in water. Now there were none. All the stars had disappeared together. The howling wind was unsettling the otherwise starless, dull evening. Anupam was having trouble finding his way. It was hazy. Even the street lights were off. Now that it was raining, he would have to use the windscreen wiper. Where did he want to go when he left home?

As the windscreen became clear, Anupam remembered that it was not only the scotch that he would find in Promila's flat, but there would be Promila too. A woman well-placed in a foreign firm, Promila Rohatgi spoke less, dressed scantily, and possessed a lively and free spirit. But no. Her cheap physicality, expensive perfumes, and her blue dreamy bedroom were too base for Anupam's taste. It would not be any different today.

It was better to go to Sougata's place; Nilabjo and others should be there. The meeting must have got over and the party was on now. Good. You can be on your own at a party. For an urban person who seeks *banaprastha*[*], a jungle of people is the best form of exile.

Banaprastha? Strange! He could not be a *banaprasthi* just because he did not entertain Promila's perverse desires! He had not even entered the *grahasthya*[*] phase yet. He was burning in endless *brahmacharya*[*]. It would be good to visit Nilabjo, Pulak, Sougata, and Ambar. They were friends.

---

[*] The third stage of the Vedic ashram system, which starts when a person hands over household responsibilities to the next generation, takes an advisory role, and gradually withdraws from the world.

[*] The second stage where a man is supposed to get married and fulfil the duties of a household as well as maintain a social life.

[*] The first stage of life or celibacy. In this stage, a student leaves home after his thread ceremony and joins a *gurukul*.

TWELVE

Anupam reached Sougata's house after the heavy rains. They were having an intense adda. Sougata worked in a reputed tobacco company. He often invited his intellectual friends over to his Alipore residence and whetted their sensibilities with rum and whiskey. He was fond of writing and occasionally wrote for the *Daily News*. He had studied English literature at Oxford; so whatever his profession might be, he had the right to consider himself as an intellectual.

Sougata had a soft, dollish wife and three round dollish daughters. Though the party was for elders and it was past ten, these cherubic girls were moving about the house with bowls filled with peanuts and potato sticks. Sougata was immensely drawn towards his plump wife and plump daughters. Anupam could not talk for more than five minutes with Arunima, Sougata's wife. Of course, Anupam realized that Arunima was a harmless creature.

As soon as he entered Sougata's house, his three dollish daughters came rolling at him like a ball, 'Anupamkaku, why are you so late? Ma, Baba, Nilabjokaku, Raokaku, they are all looking for you.'

Anupam felt highly irritated. For these children, everyone is 'kaku'*, everyone is *tumi**, the diminutive you. They did not even use the respectful form of verb while talking about elders! The children of Roy family were much more decent; they addressed elders in a more formal manner—Kakababu*. Children of the Anglo-Bengali schooling are used to this ugly practice.

Anupam wanted to say that he got late as he had to finish some work, but his throat only produced a gurgling sound.

'Oh! What happened to your voice?' the three girls chirped in a chorus. 'You must have got wet in the rains!'

Meanwhile, Sougata had come in, 'Hello! You are late!'

Anupam made a sound, '*Grrrh ghrrhghrrh.*'

'What happened? What's wrong with your voice?'

'He has lost his voice,' declared the precocious girls.

'Salt water, warm water, gargle,' suggestions started pouring in from the enthusiastic crowd.

'Gargle? Who has a throat problem?'

'Sore throat? Benzene vapour.'

'Tonsillitis? Penicillin is the answer.'

'No, you should not recommend penicillin like that. Don't you know the tragedy that befell Baby's cousin....?'

---

* An informal way of addressing uncle.
* An informal way of addressing others in second person, in Bengali.
* The more formal and respectful way of addressing uncle.

'The other day, my colleague … '

Anupam settled down beside Nilabjo on a sofa. Nilabjo, Pulak, Lalit, Sati, Ramen, Malabika, Ruma—everyone was there. Ambar was not. Anupam surveyed the room quickly. No, Kamalkali was not there. Bimal, Krishnamurthy, Mohan Rao, and Yunus sat in a circle. With their drinks in their hands, the four of them were debating excitedly on Britain's entry into the common market. Krishnamurthy was happy to see him. He pointed at Anupam and said, 'Here is a man of mature political understanding. Better ask him what its implications for common people are….' Yunus spat out a piece of tobacco of his Charminar cigarette from the tip of his tongue and said with a smile, 'Neither these journalists know anything, nor do they understand. They put down their thoughts on paper, but still do not say the truth.'

Anupam was aware that Yunus did not appreciate his latest analysis of the Bangladesh War. Anupam felt that Bangladesh had built a high structure without focusing on its foundation. Yunus had worked hard with Mujib. Why would he agree with Anupam?

'Your glass?' Bimal asked in order to divert the topic.

Anupam raised his hands to assure them.

'Rum? Whiskey?' Sougata asked.

'*Ghrrhr ghrrh*.'

'Rum?'

Anupam nodded in approval, though he did not want the rum. The questions needed to stop.

'Why are you so late?' Nilabjo asked with raised eyebrows. Anupam smiled. He felt very tired. His eyes met Ruma's as he turned. Her eyes were smiling. Her lips were always wet and shiny, as if they were licked sometime back. You could not look at them for long—it reminded one of the touch of a snake.

Ruma's smile reminded him of Kamalkali again. The wet body of Kali just after a shower.

The girls rolled towards him again, 'Kaku, what will you have? Cashew? Chips?'

Another peered over his shoulder, 'Sausage? *Dalmoot**? Please say what you will have.'

Oh! As soon as Anupam began to feel irritated, he remembered Kali's Pekinese 'darling'. He got back to his senses. Putting on an affectionate smile, he picked up a sausage with one hand and cashews with the other. He pulled the plump cheeks of the youngest girl and said, 'Thank you.'

The girl said in surprise, 'But you did not take anything from me!'

'Here. See if your drink is okay,' his host handed the glass to Anupam. 'Do you need any more ice?'

'Ice? Daddy, are you mad?' The ten-year-old girl berated her father. 'Kaku's voice is in a very dangerous state. Can't you hear? He can't even speak properly.'

---

* A spicy snack made from pulses.

'Is it that bad?' Sougata looked embarrassed. 'Say something. Let me hear how bad it is.'

Anupam felt a humorous urge inside. He started singing, 'Drink to me only with thine eyes....' Sougata shivered at the hoarseness of his voice. He said, 'Let it be. Better give it a rest, don't strain yourself.'

A debate on the Bengali novel was heating up in this corner. Pulak, Lalit, Sati, Nilabjo, and Ramen were totally into it. Subhashish was a small-time novelist himself. Ruma was his wife. They were listening quietly. Malabika, Nilabjo's non-Bengali wife, had learnt to speak in Bengali, but could not participate in these literary discussions. Ruma was anyway a person of few words. Her eyes did all the speaking. Ramen's wife, Shubha, was not in view. She was not able to attend such parties for her baby.

The modern writers were being discussed—the ones who were writing well, the ones who were promising, and those who were in the decline. Then their craft, who had mastered various schools of writing, what could have been better, native or foreign elements, pure or fake content! Everyone was all-knowing, everyone was intellectual, and everyone was a high-flying literary critique. They were not inferior to anyone in terms of their literary analysis; all of them possessed equal amount of self-respect.

Anupam did not take part in such discussions, save a few intelligent remarks on art and literature. He thought literature was out of his radar.

People hardly exposed their lack of knowledge so boldly in topics such as modern art, but they were all confident when it came to modern literature. Anupam knew his limits, so he did not want to venture beyond it. The space of literature was unprotected—or was it actually a liberated area? A free zone?

The debate continued. Now people were trying to trace the roots of the heroes of modern literature. Were they imported, or were they the illegitimate offsprings of Bengali culture, or the products of modern times? Pulak and Nilabjo were claiming that these characters were not doppelgangers of Camus, Kafka, and Sartre. Such young men were seen frequently on the streets of Kolkata. While frustration leads to revolution on one hand, it gives birth to alienation on the other. This was natural. Lalit, Sati, and Sougata's wife were of the view that these characters were not Indian. They were fake and their roots were somewhere else, because alienation could not take place in the Indian society. Both the sides were unfurling endless reasons. Anupam was not acquainted with the books and authors they were citing. His connection with Bengali literature had severed after Tarashankar*. Lalit and Sati were fighting it out with their ideals, lashing out like swords. They were very excited. Pulak and Nilabjo were no less; they were trying to portray the heroes as products of Indian realities. Ramen, almost religiously and impartially, kept on opposing both the sides. Drunk as he was, he was making explosive comments on literature.

No one was asking for Anupam's opinions, knowing that he was not much into Bengali literature. But silent waves

---

* Tarashankar Bandyopadhyay (1898–1971) was a Bengali novelist known for his depiction of social and emotional realities, especially of village life.

of words rose within his choked throat as he heard their conversations. He tried to say, 'It does not matter whether they are original or not. I have not read them, but I know these characters exist. They are Indians, sons of the soil. They are real, living right here in our country; yet, we refuse to see them. We do not want X-ray plates showing our frustration. Frustration leads to more frustration. Now we need self-respect and self-confidence. We have had our tryst with self-disgust and self-induced guilt. But no more. Now we want literature which brings positivity and hope, words which strengthen people. Unless literature is positive, you cannot build social consciousness. Self-criticism is good, but it should be constructive.'

'We need your constructive criticism,' Somshankar's words suddenly lashed his heart.

Anupam had been quiet so long. Now he turned silent from within as well. An unknown fear gripped him; he hardened and tried to resist. How was it possible? A staunch leftist, Anupam's thoughts on literature, and a staunch right-wing man, Somshankar's thoughts on political writings had an uncomfortable similarity! How was it possible?

'Why are you keeping mum?' Nilabjo thumped Anupam lightly on his back.

'My throat,' Anupam replied in a broken voice.

'Arré? Is it still sore?'

'It has worsened....'

Anupam felt like leaving the party immediately. Everyone was a littérateur, everyone was a doctor. One of them would surely suggest a homeopathic medicinc very soon. As far as a sacred cure for asthma and homeopathic medicines for sore throat was concerned, they were distributed freely by national leaders, men, women, and transgenders alike.

'You should have had Bryonia 30 earlier.'

'Vitamin C 500 would work better than that.'

Anupam had travelled quite a distance in his imagination. He tried to see Ruma's shining lips through the bottom of his empty glass. It worked as a magnifying glass—things looked much bigger. Ruma's enlarged eyes, looking bigger, were about to devour Mohan Rao.

'*Ghahahaghhhrghhar*,' Anupam was astonished. What was he trying to say amidst that meaningless banter? He perhaps wanted to say, 'Enough of it. No more. Same old stuff. Please talk about something important now. Ladies and gentlemen, time is short.'

'Kaku? You want to say something? Please take this notebook and pencil. You can write. I will show it.' Anupam saw that Sougata's daughter had got a school notebook and a red pencil for him. He ran his hands affectionately through her curly hair tied with a red ribbon. The child said cheerfully, 'You can write, okay?' Anupam took the notebook and pencil. He had something important to say. Something very vital. With the notebook open in front of him and the pencil in his hand, Anupam kept waiting.

He now tried to focus on what Krishnamurthy and others were saying. The tumultuous debate was still going on. He heard snippets and figured that their analysis had a huge flaw. They had missed out a very basic point, which was why the debate had become so prolonged. Anupam tried to explain the point quickly, '*Ghrghrghr*' (Look here, the point is simple).

'Oh, Anupamkaku! Why are you trying to talk? Write down your thoughts in the notebook,' the girl looked worried.

Anupam started to write; it was better to write down his points. Strange! After writing two pages of a point so obvious, he noticed that the girl, barely nine years old, was waiting for him to finish. Her eyes, hidden beneath her fluffy hair, were flowing with affection and sympathy for Anupam. She was patiently quiet. Anupam could see two of her newly formed teeth between her pink lips. Just like Niru's pet squirrel.

'Can I take it now?' the girl smiled as Anupam's eyes met hers. 'To whom? Bimalkaku? Raokaku? Tell me, whom should I give it to?' She lovingly placed her tiny hand on Anupam's shoulder.

Anupam suddenly started to feel nauseated. He left his notebook, tried to say 'excuse me' in that hoarse voice, and rushed towards the bathroom. Closing the bathroom door, he tried to vomit.

He was feeling very sick; a deep tremor was going through his body—*Waak*! *Waak*! He tried to throw up, a sense of discomfort in his head. He felt like screaming, 'Your honour, I am not at fault. It wasn't me ... '

Bending over the basin as he tried to vomit, Anupam broke down into tears.

THIRTEEN

It was quite late into the night. Turning on the bed switch, he sat up on the bed. A splash of yellow light made him cringe in irritation. He had gone straight to bed after returning from Sougata's place. His mother asked him to have dinner, but he declined.

He did not get back to work either. No!

He did not feel like doing anything.

He did not even feel like thinking about anything. The report on the policy of Oil Commission Subcommittee was almost ready. It had to be sent without further delay.

He did not feel like working on that report either.

Nothing felt good.

He was terribly tired and wanted to rest. But sleep did not come to him.

He went and stood silently next to his desk. His lazy eyes browsed through the papers and books, the walls hidden beneath the books. Which book should he read now? Which one? His eyes stopped at *Resurrection*, an adolescent favourite. But he pulled his hand back. What if he did not like it anymore? He tried to look at other books. A new, abridged version of *Asian Drama* had come out. Should he flip through it? No, let it be.

Anupam opened the drawer and took out the long brown envelope. People did not send personal letters in such envelopes. They sent applications in them. Or bills. He opened the envelope with his sleepless, tired fingers, without using a letter opener, and then sat in the armchair. A lot of paper. A bunch of foolscap pages.

The letters were in black ink, neatly written in Bengali. The date was mentioned on the left-hand corner. An enormous portion of the top, the bottom, and the left margins were left empty. Each paper had a different date. There were no signatures.

Just like confessions in a diary.

Sudha had sent him such letters earlier as well. She was in Midnapore for a few months while working on a research project. That time, Sudha's letters were vastly different from the way she spoke. She was rough, headstrong, and bold when she spoke; her letters were just the opposite. He did not like Sudha's words; they were too wild, too audacious. He disliked her letters even more. They were wilder. Lurking in the light and shadow of nature and the powerful ebb and flow of primal life, Sudha's letters got into terrains prohibited by Anupam, areas where he threatened to prosecute trespassers.

He did not read these letters for the past three days. He just did not muster the courage to do so.

Since Sudha returned from Midnapore, Anupam had behaved in such a way that someone as untamed as Sudha even gave up. She moved to South India with a new job.

'You will like working on the new project. Professor Ramalingam is a great person,' Anupam had said. 'Also, Osmania University has a very nice campus. Send an application. Fast.'

'But my research?' Sudha wailed.

'You can continue to work under Ramalingam if you want.'

'So you really want to drive me away?'

'How strange! Why should I drive you away? Listen, Sudha, you do not possess the academic temperament. This kind of applied research is good for you. Calm down and send an application. I better write a letter of recommendation for you.'

'Okay. When will you give me the recommendation letter?'

'Not tomorrow. I will be busy at Kamalkali's place. Better come day after. Or just send your brother or anybody else to collect it.'

Anupam said this while signing a few notices. When he looked up, Sudha had gone.

She never came back.

Anupam had prepared a recommendation letter for her. Sudha did not come to collect it. He got to know from others that she had shifted to Hyderabad.

They met, nonetheless, at the interview board. Sudha was on the other side of the table. Anupam was on this side with Sabarwal and Mangeshkar. He did not ask her questions, since she was his student. Sudha responded to all the questions, maintaining eye contact with him. She looked unabashedly proud and confident. That was the last time. They never met again.

She got a job even without the recommendation of Anupam.

This is the first letter. Almost after three months. Switching on the table lamp, he opened the bunch of papers in front of him.

(Sudha's letters)

24.04

Yearning for you. Darling, missing you terribly. Here, the train is running through an endless bridge, shaking the depths of darkness. The void beneath my feet is echoing around—robust. Sometimes, it is playing a sweet domestic rhyme, like anklets of household chores. The sudden flashes of lights from the runaway platforms are piercing my eyes. The snake charmer's tune is crushing my heart every moment. It is revolving around me in memory and slipping away. My imagination is rising like a snake's head, the jewel of secret desire flashing on it ...

Darling, I am leaving.

Can you hear me? I am going away.

25.04

The upper bunk feels like a tiny room. Just the two of us. The floor, far far below, is shivering and rushing to catch up. But how can it keep up with the bunk? This berth is like a magic carpet. It has flown me to you. You and me. You are sitting on the easy chair, contemplating about the next day's lecture or typing out the piece for the next 'Roy's Corner'. I am standing next to you, leaning over you with my hands resting on the armrests of your chair. My breasts guard your prized brain, et cetera. I can see some of your hairs greying. Yes, darling, yours too. The body is unsparing when it comes to paying a price for your age—forty has not spared you—no, forty-five—or one hundred and forty-five? Darling, as you grow old, I will grow a little older. Because I have my feet firmly on the ground. You are too much of a coward. You are scared of the reality just like a child. You dress up as an adult tyrant, make up with fake beards and moustaches, but you are a child inside. When you are alone, you don't even let your limbs come close to your heart, lest they get to know the dilemmas inside. Sudha has got to know everything, no matter what you do or what you say. Sudha has heard the music of the secret instrument in your heart.

It doesn't matter whether the train is running or not, whether the night is passing or not, whether the scenery outside the windows are changing or not. Nothing matters. This journey is never going to end. I will keep going far away, and farther away, so far that the distance will be endless.

Dearest, my dearest no one, my treasure, the apple of my eyes—I offer you these nights, these sounds, this silence, this impenetrable loneliness, this suffocation, this freedom, this purity, this slumber, along with a cluster of dim stars. All yours. You may take them or reject, but all is yours. This pace, this sole obligatory melancholia, all yours. Me, the only gravitational force in this orbit—all yours.

The fingers of my hand, the tip of my tongue, my nipples, are dying to write this love letter to you. They are so deft in creating love letters. But darling, will you be able to read that letter? You do not know how to read such letters. Dawn will break soon. I have to stop and get off. I so want to scream and jump out of the train and be crushed by these soulless wheels, this body of much desire and shame be crushed. This raw, 153 cm bundle of 110 pound flesh, bones, liver and fat; blind, insensate, deaf and dumb, sensual—that which has confused you, that which has lost you, should be destroyed.

Where is the train heading to? Towards you, irrespective of any direction it is taking. Because all directions are your directions, and I continue to be towards you.

20.05

Good that I came here. You cannot flee from this place. There you are, driving this bullock cart in a green shirt. I am drawing water from the well in a golden pitcher, wearing a red ghaghra.*

* A long, flowing skirt worn by women in parts of India.

02.06

I keep feeling that I will receive a letter from you. When in office, I hope I will go home and get a letter. At home, I dream of receiving your letter in office. But I know you do not even know my address. I wonder if you know my name.

There are no known faces here, no shades of familiar trees or known crossroads. Here there is only work, work, and work. And when I don't have work, only you, you, and you.

08.06

My heart is filled all the time, as if a river is flowing through. Like you feel when your breasts well up with milk. Is this how you feel when your breasts are filled with milk? Like an accomplishment or a revelation. Time is running like steam launch cutting through a still lake—the waves are making ripples and crashing down on the bank just like snakes' strike. Should I thank you for this?

12.06

As I close my eyes—the surreal meadows. The star-studded ceiling. Moon-warmed moments running through my pulse. The sky-river, the moon inside my palm, the moon on my lap, powdered moon in the clothes, moon's nectar inside the blouse. Endless tears in the air, this earth which is awaiting, bless it more beauty—is this love? Darling, believe me, that is love. Only one evening, just one evening, that was your only true moment—trust me, that was your truth, your victory. That is your love.

You consider yourself very wise. But you know nothing. You have learnt nothing from life. That evening that you consider was your moment of defeat—the shame of which you want to erase through this war with Sudha—was actually the moment of your resurrection.

Your face looked so pallid on the day of the interview. I could see through your blank white eyes. Those were your fake moustache and beard. That is my victory. Darling, that is your sorrow. That is your love.

Anupam removed his glasses as he finished reading up till here. He then covered the letters with a book. He saw that there were still two more pages of the letter to be read. Then he took all the pages, including the two unread ones, folded them, and put them back inside the envelope. He lightly held the envelope with three fingers of each palm and very carefully tore Sudha's letters to bits. Even before the last part was read, it was tattered into a hundred pieces. Crushing the pieces within his fist, he shaped the mangled remains of the letter into a strong cannon ball.

Putting it back on the table, he picked up a covered glass of water. The coaster on the glass had 'Anu' engraved on it. This vessel had been a part of his life since his adolescence.

He got it as a gift in his thread ceremony.* He never noticed that the glass was made of silver. He overlooked this even now. He gave up his thread after he boarded the ship towards the West. But he had not been able to do away with the gifts that he had received in the ceremony.

He wanted to quench his thirst with a glass of water. Gulping down the water in one breath, he picked up the clump of torn pages. It was aimed accurately at the wastepaper basket kept in a corner of the room. It flew—the ball like a bird's egg—straight into the centre of the basket with a gentle, soft noise.

Feeling satisfied with his aim, Anupam went to bed. In a moment, he turned off the bed switch and sealed the dense, silent, and desolate darkness in the room.

---

*A religious ceremony of introducing an adolescent boy into Brahminhood with the sacred thread.

FOURTEEN

The doctor's chamber was crowded. In spite of a prior appointment, Anupam had been waiting for twenty-five minutes after submitting a slip. He had not been called yet. Magazines stacked on the table, *Shankar's Weekly, The Illustrated Weekly of India*, even *Filmfare*, had all been checked. The Bengali weeklies were left. With nothing else to do, Anupam picked up one of those.

He read through the editorial casually. Not bad. Quite sensible and controlled. Lucid, sharp, and substantial. He was disappointed while going through the poems. It was a pity that people were still writing such silly slush on women, rivers, and leaves. Were they even being published? Especially when the country was going through such troubled times! The illustration of the short story suggested that it was a romantic one. Anupam could not read sugary love stories any more. He went through the section on literary criticism too. As Anupam was comparing his current read with English papers, judging their standards thoroughly, he sometimes raised his eyebrows, sometimes wrinkled his nose. Suddenly, one of the pages caught his attention. It was nothing but an episode from a novel published serially—a father making his son learn a prayer.

He was saying, 'Recite in the morning, recite throughout the day. After a while, it will be etched into your soul.'

Gongs and bells of prayer from the Roy household reverberated somewhere deep inside Anupam's heart. The sacred thread slung across his father's chest, the marks of sandal pasted on his fair body after he came back from a bath in the Ganga—Baba used to spend most of the day in the family temple. When Anu and Niru played in the courtyard, Baba recited his prayers in the morning and in the evening—throughout the day, all the time. The lines were supposed to be etched into his heart. But did they get etched into his soul?

Anupam tried to read the prayer on print, 'I am beyond anger, beyond ego. I am never indolent, I am above sensory pleasures ... ' It was as if Krishnachaitanya Roy's deep, self-absorbed voice wafted in from another lifetime: '*Adveṣṭa sarva-bhutanam/ maitraḥ karuṇa eva ca/ nirmamo nirahankaraḥ/ sama-duḥkha-sukhaḥ kṣami*.' The weekly was left open on his lap. Anupam did not read it anymore. He was transported to his childhood, listening to his father reading the Gita in their family courtyard: '*Santuṣṭaḥ satatam yogi yatatma dṛḍha-niscayaḥ*.' Oh! What a strange man! Krishnachaitanya spent the entire day in the prayer room, but everyone knew the person that he was within. Did Anupam not know the abuses hurled by his jethima? Did he not overhear the horrible exchange between Binu jhi, the family's maid, and his cousin's sister-in-law? Everyone knew that his deep religiosity and piousness was actually a cover-up, like a bra camouflaging the inner emptiness. *Hypocrisy, thy name is religion*. And then, Anupam could hear that hypocrite man's deep voice again, just as one hears the distant sound of waves through a conch shell, '*Bhaktiman, yah, sa me priyah*. Anu, you cannot find what you love unless you are pious. If you want God to love you, you have to be selfless, you have to remain unmoved by praise or criticism. *Anapeksah sucir daksa udasino gata-vyathah*—you cannot feel pain in times of shame and admonition, sorrows and insult. Anu, my son, everything in life depends on practice.'

Anupam now felt a strong urge to throttle the voice of that cheat, that imposter, the skilled actor who faked his piousness. Tormented inside, he tried to go through the flurry of words in the magazine calmly.

'Dr Anupam Roy?' the bearer asked.

'Practice devotion, Anu. Try to be humble, be more tolerant than trees, be more grounded than grass. Be respectful, give up on ego, you will experience God's mercy.'

'I think it is easy for any intelligent man to be more tolerant than trees, but it is harmful to be more grounded than grass, that humble. It is the duty of a well-mannered person to treat others respectfully, but to give up on ego? Is that possible at all? Other than saints?'

Anupam was busy talking to himself. It was impossible to be beyond sorrow if you lived in a society. You are not lazy, you are determined. But are you clean, Anupam? How can Krishnachaitanya's son be clean? How can he be pure just by memorizing legends, the legend of Pundarikaksha? Blood spoke, Anupam's blood, and so did his chromosome.

A man whose family heirloom was hypocrisy, could he ever be pure?

'Is Anupam Roy here? Dr Anupam Roy?'

'Yes, I am Anupam Roy.'

'It's your turn now. Come.'

Anupam kept the magazine back and picked up his briefcase. He looked at his watch. The doctor had delayed his appointment by forty-five minutes straight.

He greeted the doctor as he entered his chamber. Dr Banerjee placed his hands on Anupam's forehead and said in a professional tone, 'Have a seat. Tell me, what is your complaint? What problem are you facing?'

The doctor forced a smile and said, 'Not to worry! Don't be so depressed. Nothing fatal has happened, right? But yes, your profession might be affected a bit. Thank God that you are not a singer!' He extended his hands towards Anupam. 'In any case,' he warmly pressed Anupam's nervous palms and said, 'your actual work, writing, will not be hampered at all.'

Anupam shivered and pulled his hand away. He could never tolerate affectionate gesture from a man. When he touched his father's feet, he would place his hand lovingly on Anupam's head for some time and recite a few blessings. His uncle did not observe such rituals.

The doctor was slightly surprised, 'What are you afraid of? In Vienna, you can get better treatment for this condition.

They have provisions for operations. You keep travelling to different countries. Why don't you get the surgery done in Vienna?'

'Doctor, are you trying to say that I am going lose my voice forever?'

'Well ... in a way ... ultimately, umm ... I am afraid....' He then spoke on quite normally, in a lighter note. 'Replacement of voice box is not a big deal nowadays. It will not be your normal voice, but you will manage. You can say everything—with a simple and scientific false voice.' The doctor picked up the envelope and put it in the drawer.

'Remember, smoking is deadly for you. One chord is permanently damaged and the other is almost gone. You people ruin your throats with smoke. Calcutta is anyway highly polluted. Breathing in this city is equal to smoking twenty cigarettes a day.'

Anupam's eyes took a quick tour of the lighter and a pack of Vazi cigarettes kept on the table. He wore a smile, 'Doctor, for how long will I be unable to talk?'

'Don't talk. Not at all. Do you remember that Gandhiji used to spend a day without talking every week? You do exactly the same. But seven days in a week. Don't leave your house in the next three weeks. Your voice needs complete rest.'

'That means I will not be able to talk at all? It's gone? A permanent loss?'

'Arré! No. Is that what I said? Just don't talk for three weeks. I think you have to get the surgery done. But, why worry? Get these Macrabin and vitamin injections for three weeks and this steroid and antibiotic for ten days, just as I have mentioned in the prescription. And give your voice a complete rest. Okay? See me after three weeks. Umm ... okay? Achcha?' The finality in the tone was as distinct as Somshankar's. The doctor rang the bell on the table. He looked relieved as his job with this patient was over.

'Thank you, Doctor.'

'Welcome. Next!'

Anupam came out of the clinic and checked his watch. He was still in Park Street. It would be good to eat something. Kamalkali would come to Flurys at four-thirty. There was enough time. This was lunch hour—it would be crowded everywhere. There was no question of delivering lectures. Even speaking was forbidden. He would better go to the restaurant.

'It would be nice to visit the newspaper house,' Anupam thought after ordering coffee and sandwiches. Sanjeeb came in the morning, but he could not give him the edited piece. This was the first exception in six years—this week's 'Roy's Corner' would not be published.

But he could still write it here in a couple of hours. His order had not arrived yet. No problem even if it came now. After Anupam took out his notepad and pen, he remembered that he had to call Ma too. She would not eat otherwise!

It was painful to talk, even though he spoke very little. Ma was hard of hearing and Anupam, too, could not speak properly these days.

The coffee soothed his throat. What a comforting moment! The cold room was cooling his body, while the drink was warming him inside. This was what you called sensory pleasure.

He uncapped his pen. Let's see. He who makes a disabled person climb a mountain also throws a mad elephant into a ditch—'*yatatma drranishchayay*'—but being a determined soul, he can surely come out of the ditch all by himself.

The piece was ready after a bit of effort. This time, his focus was not on his own nation—he borrowed a few points from the report on oil crisis and fleshed out enough matter for two columns. Suddenly, he felt drained and exhausted.

After paying the bill, he was out on the streets again. Now he needed brandy, not the stale old coffee. His throat pained. After this, he would have to submit the essay, although it had not been typed yet. Let Kamalkali come. Then he would give it.

He saw Ramen the moment he walked into the bar. Ramen, Mahinder, Subhashish, and a few untidy drunkards were there. Must be artists or painters, or some author of sorts. Anupam did not feel like talking to them today. He hadn't been feeling too well. So he walked towards a different table.

But Ramen came running to him, his arms wide open, 'Arré, arré! Big brother!' he squealed in delight. 'Come, come. We are waiting for you. Please deliver some free knowledge. Some lessons on morals. Please....'

Anupam stood still. All his senses grew sharper. He also applied his sixth sense to get a hang of Ramen's mood. Hot air blew out of his ears. Ramen generally spoke to him with respect and distance, and always added a 'babu' after his name. He never called him 'brother', no matter how tipsy he was.

'Come, Bro. Sit here. Tell us what your parents told you. You won't? Why? Angry about something? Let me tell you, then,' his speech slurred. 'Parents have asked you to go bar-hopping during the day in your car and have fun with women in the evening. If you find some time, then squeeze in some long lectures to send cherubic boys to the torture chamber and keep a safe distance so that you can run away whenever required. This is true, isn't it? Say it, swine! Isn't it true? Come, you rascal! I will teach you a good intellectual lesson. I will put an end to your fancy craving for revolution—liar, dishonest, imposter, foreign money launderer, murderer, hypocrite—'

Ramen's head drooped as he tried to get up. Subhashish, Mahinder, and a few other dishevelled men had got him. Even the bearers rushed towards him. He had hurled the liquor-filled glass at Anupam. Missing its target, it shattered against the wall. The shards spread all over, the air smelling heavy with liquor.

Ramen was listless with his head on the table. His fiery, piercing gaze was now mellowed behind his sleeves.

Subhashish walked shyly towards Anupam and whispered something into his ears.

It was as if Anupam's legs had grown into the floor like old roots. But he was not a tree. How could he draw life force through his feet from the ground? He tried hard to press on his intelligence; it kept slipping from his hands like the doors of a moving train. The noise of the breaking glass echoed across the deaf caves inside.

In the midst of all this, Anupam could faintly hear someone muttering a few words at a distance, like a taped message in a telephone:

'Don't mind, Anupamda. Ramen is not in his senses today—Somen's dead body was discovered in the Ganga this morning. It must be someone from the party who did this.'

FIFTEEN

Anupam managed to keep his appointment for tea with Kamalkali at Flurys, but he was slightly delayed. Though he went there, he could not talk at all. He also wanted to submit his piece at the newspaper office. Even if his first write-up was not ready, he had written something new. There was no point in not submitting it now. There was no harm in writing about the outside world for a while. He had indeed written about the world outside instead of his native land. But his hands were tied by some anti-force within him. Even if the material for 'Roy's Corner' was ready, this was the first time it did not hit the press.

Some time after the glass was flung at him, Anupam had left that place and went straight to the banks of Ganga.

For the past three months, he had been aware that Ramen's younger brother was missing. So this was the news—his body had been found.

Anupam bought a packet of Gold Flake cigarettes and a matchbox from a small shop. He hardly remembered what Dr Banerjee had said a couple of hours back. He did not smoke much, and was barely addicted to anything apart from tea and coffee. His greatest addiction was to be not enslaved by any kind of addiction.

But today, as he sat on a concrete bench under a spreading, old peepul tree by the tranquil riverside, Anupam was smoking one cigarette after another. Unending rings of smoke covered his eyes, nose, and face—as if an unquenchable fire had broken out inside.

Anupam Roy's eyes looked around blankly. He tried to free his mind—but could you really do it? Looking vacantly, he tried to declutter his mind. How to go about it? Where to look? What to do? What could one do to avoid all kinds of thoughts? *'Nainam chindanti sastrani nainam dahati pavakah'*—ah! Was there no respite from the memories of Roy Mansion? Were memories indestructible? Though it was said that the loss of memory equalled to the loss of the mind, but, sometimes, if you did not wipe out memories, there was a possibility of your intelligence being wiped out altogether. Loss of intelligence led to destruction—that was the ultimate truth.

Anupam's eyes tried to cajole his troubled soul. He looked at the boats sailing through the river. Boats with shades, without shades, speedboats, ferryboats, steamers sailing towards the sea, steamers sailing upstream. Thin, large, loaded, empty. A small foreign ship had been anchored at a distance. It was named after this distant continent. What was it doing here, in the saffron waters of the Hooghly? They were not related at all, but the ship had blissfully surrendered itself unto this river.

As Anupam shifted his gaze from the water towards the sky, the rays of the setting sun blinded him for a moment. He covered his eyes with his hand, trying to save them from the glowing light. Silken rings of orange bloomed like stemless flowers, one after another, in an ocean of darkness. Gradually, the orange flowers transformed into ripe fruits, then into unripe ones, and then into glowing green sparks. Finally, they changed into rows of blue gems. Anupam removed his hand from his eyes and found a lonely, adamant kite floating round in circles in the sky. Imprisoned within a circular trap of stubbornness, the kite centring around the void was creating circle after circle.

Einstein, while explaining the Theory of Relativity, had once commented that the hour before the arrival of one's beloved is infinite (like Draupadi's saree), but even three hours after the lover's arrival, it flies by so fast (like uncovered camphor).

But Anupam's experience was different on that day.

Kamalkali was already waiting when Anupam arrived. Slightly annoyed at his delay, her lips were pouted. In a fiery chiffon saree with a matching blouse, she looked stunning. Her puffed-up hair shrouded her face and neck like thick clumps of smoke, all over her forehead, shoulders, and chest. Anupam realized that this metaphor of smoke and flowers was not his own. It was a classic found in the work of the master of metaphors, Kalidasa. But the ones who called him the master of metaphors did not know about the all-time master of metaphor, William Shakespeare.

A flash of self-hatred swept over him suddenly.

'Are you still going to be in love with your slyly refined aesthetics, Anupam?'

Kamalkali's hand on the table, smooth and creamy, was as delicious as the cherry cake beside it. The red nail paint and the diamond ring adorning her finger made her look crisp and enticing. But Anupam did not feel like touching her at all. Kamalkali's *anchal* kept falling off the right places, but Anupam's eyes came back to his teacup.

His throat was not producing any sound at all. Two more cigarettes were left in the packet. Kamalkali was used to having a mercurial, fancy banter with Anupam. She looked bored too.

There was an invisible glass wall between the two. You could see the other from one side, but could hear nothing. Not working at all—a bell rang in his heart.

'Not fair. Look at you. Invited me here and not saying a word.'

'*Ghhrrrr*...?' (I am really sorry....)

'That's okay, you are in pain! Better let me talk. Listen. See the point is ... what to say.'

The order for food and drinks was placed. Kamalkali, in a molten state of sympathy, looked wistfully at Anupam. He enjoyed it. She soon found a topic for discussion.

'We had a women's cooperative meeting here, at Park Hotel, today. We have organized a charity lunch for Mother Teresa. There will be 200 seats, just for twenty-five rupees each and fifty rupees for a double seat. Please purchase a double seat, will you?'

Anupam made an approving gesture and wore a pleasant, sociable smile. He moved his lips as if to say, 'Of course, of course.' This assurance did not translate to any kind of sound anywhere in the world.

'Thank you. There is time. This is on the second Saturday next month. It is difficult to arrange such events on Sundays, as people go for races then.'*

Anupam nodded sympathetically, like a thinker addressing the gravity of the situation.

'Anapeksha shuchirdaksh udasina gatavyatha'—Am I pure? Who is pure? Somen? Samir? What does *anapeksha* mean? Continuing with one's work without thinking of the outcome? That is how saints work. Every deed has an outcome—you should not be the one to enjoy its consequences.

'I am interviewing Mother Teresa for the *Adam and Eve* magazine. We booked an appointment for next week. Shireen Dalmootwala and me. Both of us will be writing the feature.'

Oh! I invited this deadly meeting for myself! How will I break free from Kamalkali's chatter? Good that the teapot is empty now. I should leave without getting a refill.

'Please suggest a few questions for Mother Teresa. Okay, you do not need to talk now. Please think about it and prepare a questionnaire for me at leisure. After all, Mother Teresa is a twentieth-century saint. Her interview has to come out well.

---

* Taking part in horse racing and gambling has been a very popular pastime among the upper-class population in Calcutta.

A twentieth-century saint. It is a new fad—statements like these. But do saints belong to centuries? Saints are beyond death, but not beyond pain. You cannot be a saint if you are beyond pain. The quality of a saint is to feel pain. A saint's heart contains fathomless sense of pain and endless forbearance. I am no saint. I can't.

'Let's go and watch the sunset by the river,' Kali said in the car. A note went wrong with the proposition. A sharp blade of light adorned Kamalkali's breasts—the last flash of the setting sun. He thought of a headless chicken being roasted. His eyes looked for some shade. Tender bunches of fruits beneath her blouse peeped out, the way ripe oranges peek out of baskets in Sealdah bazaar. Anupam's steering found its way towards the riverside.

But there stood the stone statue of a thin man, holding a long stick and standing over an insanely high pedestal with one of his feet forward.

Facing the guarding, semi-naked figure of Gandhi, Anupam's steering changed its direction again.

'Are you not going to the Ganga?'

Anupam Roy lightly pressed his finger to his throat. He tried to express the pain through his eyes. Anupam shook his head helplessly. Although unwilling, he, almost brutally, had to control himself just because of his throat pain—Kamalkali's innocent mind had no doubt about it.

'Poor thing!' Her red lips parted like a cherry fruit in sympathy. The fruit split open. Through the crack, Anupam could see Kali's pristine teeth and pink tongue making bubbles of words like *'tsk ... tsk'*. Such a scene, such a sound turned on the tired, male body of Anupam.

Just then, he remembered that this was the same way in which Kali called her Pekinese dog.

The car picked up speed along with Anupam's pulse. He started talking to himself once he came back to his senses, 'Drive slow, Anupam. In fact, you don't have any destination. Lower your speed. No harm if you get slightly late or fall behind. Calm down, Anupam, be composed.'

SIXTEEN

After seeing off Kamalkali unceremoniously, Anupam got home and called out to Keshto. His voice sounded terrible; both Keshto and Anupam himself got scared.

'What did the doctor say, Dadababu? Your voice seems to have gotten worse.'

'I have to go again.'

'Chorda came to take Ma home. She has prepared your tiffin. Let me get it for you.'

Anupam shook his head in denial and went to the cabinet. He took out a bottle of Coronation Whiskey he brought from Bhutan, and got some cold soda from the fridge. Ice? Better not. He chose a crystal glass.

What a waste the day was! A whole working day wasted! Only his piece was ready, but he did not submit it. He stood up and dialled a number. As soon as *Daily News* answered his call, he asked for Mukherji. But the person on the other side kept saying, 'Hello, hello, whom do you want to speak to? Who you are looking for?' Anupam repeated again. The person on the other side remained deaf and disconnected the phone.

Tired, Anupam returned to his sofa. Keshto stood behind him.

'You could not place the call?' he asked. 'You want to telephone? Should I try?'

Yes, Anupam thought for a moment. Keshto could talk in Bengali and inform Mukherji. They could send a peon to collect the article. Then he thought that Keshto could go and submit the letter himself. He was excited at the thought of being left on his own for an hour at least.

He signalled Keshto to bring his briefcase. Keshto brought it to him.

He took out the writing and quickly glanced through it once. It was fine. He wrote the address on the envelope and gave it to Keshto. Keshto checked the address and said, 'This is why you called? I finished cooking in the morning itself. I will go and give it.'

'Roy's Corner' would not be stopped. It would be published this week too. Anupam felt a sense of relief. Really, how could he think of stopping it? Could there be any connection between the problem in 'Roy's Corner' and Somen's death? There could be no connection.

Anupam tried to train his mind, 'Don't think of Samir. Think of other things.' Keshto had shut the door before going out. The house was empty. 'Whom should I think about?' Not Kali. Nalini Deshpande? Shobhana Dasgupta? Ruma, Subhashish's wife? They got torridly close after attending a new year's party all night, he and Ruma. He avoided Ruma since then. Her shiny wet lips, her liquid eyes filled with unreal words—he was scared of them all.

And he was scared of Sudha too—her ordinary sarees, her torn Kolhapuri sandals, her piercing gaze, and her whip-like plaits. Sudha pretended to see through his past and future as she played with her plaits. She had to be dealt with cautiously, like a loaded gun. Even if you were thinking of Sudha, you needed to be careful.

Guns! Is Samir in prison? Anupam would appoint a lawyer for him. Samir must not have taken any lives himself. Surely not. Not Samir, at least. But it was often that such boys took the wrong path. The path of hatred was many times delusional.

Sudha said, 'Why quite often? Are you deliberately choosing to keep it vague?' The inner voice of Anupam threw a remark, 'Or is it academic hesitation? If he considers their path wrong, why will he help them? Is it just the milk of human kindness?'

Anupam thought—no, not actually so. He was politically sympathetic towards them for sure. He accepted their method, as he supported their main objective. Be it revolution or life, there could be nothing totally non-violent. There were two separate entities: necessary violence and unnecessary violence. It was not purely attachment; he had believed in the movement too.

Sudha said, 'You believed in it in the past. Not anymore? Why did you remain mum when Somshankar Duttaray said, "We know that you just feel for the miserable students, not for their politics." Why didn't you protest then?' The voice inside Anupam started off again, 'The nerve to speak the truth is actual courage. You considered that to be audacity.

That's the reason you kept mum. You remember what Jesus said to Peter?' Sudha said, 'You are fond of hard measures!'

'Ah, Sudha, can you please be quiet? You talk too much. You are too bold. You say exactly what you think; your tongue and your heart are always bare. The covering for the mind and the heart is called civility, Sudha. If we show everything to the world, it is as bad as roaming naked. Then why do we wear clothes? There should some kind of garb for the body as well as for our words.'

Anupam went to the table to refill his glass. The report for UN Oil Subcommittee was lying on the desk. It had to be completed today. He sat at the typewriter after filling his glass. He was getting distracted by weird thoughts; it would be much better to put his mind through a set regimen.

No sooner did he sit at the typewriter than he got a call. He had to leave the desk again. It was good that no guests had dropped by yet. He kept saying 'hello' over the phone. It did not yield any results. On the other side, his brother kept saying, 'Dada dada.' Anupam exerted all his force and said, 'Niruuuu.' Niru could not hear. Irritated to the core, Anupam kept down the receiver beside the phone. Good riddance, no more calls now.

He must fix an appointment with Dr Roychoudhury today itself. He had a long waiting list. A second opinion was required, but the check-up could not be delayed anymore. He did not like worrying too much about his body. Illnesses were common. He was lucky enough to be in the best health so far. This was just a hitch. Not bad. He was in his mid-forties.

Anupam was jolted. Mid-forties. Forty-five? Was he that old? His father had died when he was forty-five. But his father Krishnachaitanya Roy was not a young man like him. He was an old man with a strong, religious bent of mind. An adolescent Anupam got to know about his youthful urges quite clearly though. When the two-day-old news of his father's death reached London through the fixed template of a telegram, Anupam was a little overwhelmed at the beginning, but felt a strange sense of freedom as well. He felt deeply satisfied thinking that all those who sinned in their lifetime were met with natural justice. 'Rightly served,' he had thought then.

But his mother? Grandmother? What did they do to face sorrow of such magnitude? Did it have to do with karma? Even they had committed sins. Anupam questioned all of them in his imaginary court on a damp and cold afternoon in London. Though he used words like 'vice' and 'virtue', he was not thinking in terms of typical religious beliefs, but in terms of basic good and evil. He judged his elders through humanitarian values. Yes, Ma was at fault, and so was his grandmother. It was a sin to give leverage to a criminal. One got punished in court for that. Belarani and Charuhashini deserved the grief. The punishment for great sin was great grief.

Anupam was born when Krishnachaitanya was twenty-two. Krishnachaitanya died when Anupam was twenty-three. Anupam was curious about one, and only one mysterious decision that his father took. In a family where all children were named after the family deity, his father broke the tradition and chose to call him Anupam. But there was a touch of Lord Krishna in his name—Anupamkrishna.

Aligning with that, his brother was named Nirupamkrishna. Anupam removed 'Krishna' from his name when he entered college. In all his official papers, one alphabet signified the presence of Krishna in his name—'K'. He was Anupam K. Roy. The initials of his middle name questioned his identity, the letter 'K' sounding like 'Ke' in Bengali, meaning 'who'.

Krishnachaitanya used to be engrossed in worship. *Namkirtan**, Gita *path**, fasts, rituals—there was something or the other all the time. His uncle Krishnagovinda was one of the prominent criminal lawyers in Calcutta. It was strange how a person from a Vaishnava family could exercise so much power. Ruffians and killers paid regular visits to their house. Even so many years back, his uncle charged a thousand rupees per meeting. He named his sons Govinda Vijay, Madhava Vijay, and Keshava Vijay. His uncle earned a lot and spent even more. No one considered him an exemplary Vaishnava. He was hardly seen at pujas, except for the ones arranged by Anupam's grandmother.

Jethima was just the opposite. She was a bag of rituals. Widowhood had made her increasingly maniac, diseased, and, of course, bitter. The solitary reason for her frustration was because Anupam's father did nothing and made his brother shoulder the responsibility of his wife and sons. A useless man, Anupam's father spent the entire day in the prayer room. Even so, he was not a pure and honest soul. Everyone knew where his mind actually was. For Jethima, even Anupam's mother was full of flaws. She was the wife

---

* Day-long recital of verses sung in praise of God.
* Readings from the Gita.

of a pseudo-religious man of questionable character. She had supposedly indulged her husband and did not show any speck of gratitude or respect towards their benefactor, her brother-in-law. Jethima spent her days trying to exact gratitude for her husband's deeds.

Later, Anupam got to know that his brother, he, and his parents had equal rights in the house where they were living a life of humiliation. They had rights over the food and shelter that they were provided grudgingly. The property was equally owned by his father and his uncle, and the household was run on that money. His uncle's earnings were spent abroad, deposited in the bank, converted to Jethima's jewellery, and spent in three sons and seven daughters' education and marriage. Ma knew all this, but she never resisted Jethima's torture and insult. Granted that beneath his religious fanaticism, his father was a hypocrite. But why hadn't Ma ever protested? How could one justify such unquestioning loyalty? This put a dog's faith towards its master to shame.

Anupam undoubtedly believed that the imposter Krishnachaitanya Roy was solely responsible for his mother's miseries. It was for him that Khemodashundori treated Belarani like a criminal.

He had had a clear idea of human nature since childhood. Proudly so. This was the resource he had used to conduct himself wisely throughout his life. He never had to try too hard. Everything in his life had been organized exactly as he had wanted. Be it the way Maria stepped aside, or the way Sudha was made to leave for Hyderabad.

This did not work in Samir's case. It was about to turn faulty with Sudha, but Anupam averted the mistake at the right stage, thanks to his intelligence.

Anupam believed that intelligent people did not need God. Had Krishnachaitanya been as shrewd as Krishnagovinda, he would not turn to God at every step. Anupam respected his uncle. He depended on his intelligence to sail through life. Since he was successful in this, old age could not dampen his confidence. Even when his sport with intelligence in court got over due to his age, he did not turn to God and religion for respite.

Krishnachaitanya, on the other hand, as far as Anupam's memory went back, was always seen with sandalwood pasted on his forehead, the eternal devotee ...

Icy rain, accompanied by a hostile sharp wind, sliced through London's flesh and blood that day. The grey, smoke-laden air was such that it could make one feel desolate in a crowd. After receiving the telegram that pale afternoon, Anupam was out in the slushy streets looking for his friends. He wore galoshes to shield his expensive shoes. The pubs would not open before six at evening. He sat with his friends at Joe Walter's place. His friends Joe, Kenneth, and Jeffrey wanted to know what they were celebrating over drinks. Anupam spoke about some good news from home. His family has won a difficult legal case. They partied late into the night; after six, they went to Soho Square for pubcrawling. The four of them had a lot of fun, meticulously checking out the photographs of nude women outside the nightclubs after the pubs got closed.

SEVENTEEN

Maria got very busy with 'Roy' that night. They had been in a relationship for two years and it was quite serious. Maria's overcaring attitude had already begun to prick him. Maria's 'Roy'. She would say, 'Anupam, whichever way I try to shorten your name, it will sound like a girl's name—either Ann or Pam. It is far better to call you Roy. That sounds like a man's name.'

After celebrating his father's death over food and drinks, as the night got deeper and the loneliness grew more intense, Anupam sought shelter in Maria's arms. He cried profusely in the warmth of her soft bosoms. No, he was not crying for Krishnachaitanya. Instead, he remembered Fulkaki. There was a strange fragrance in Maria's breasts that day, something special in the touch of her fingers. Maria turned into Fulkaki* after reading the telegram. Like a child, Anupam was crying in his Fulkaki's arms. Thus, the elder son of the deceased Krishnachaitanya Roy, Anupamkrishna Roy, fell into a deep intoxicated sleep on a Jewish woman Maria Epstein's bed, far away from any kind of post-death rituals.

---

* Kaki implies the wife of the younger brother of one's father.

Forty-five years—the thought of these words evoked so many memories! No, not before the typewriter, not here. Bring yourself back, Anupam!

'Fulkaki'—the name affected the very root of his nervous system and dealt a strong, impactful blow. Whenever he remembered this name, a deep, heavy echo reverberated within him.

However, Maria.

'Maria'—the name made Anupam uncomfortable in his guts. It sent a tremor of terror through his body.

Anupam, calm down.

After uncovering the typewriter, Anupam stared at the virgin space on the papers and composed himself. He again calculated—if he did not post the article in a couple of days, there would be no time left to make stencil copies for distribution before the conference.

If his throat's condition did not improve, there was no use going to attend the meeting in the first week of the next month. But he cancelled his visit to Geneva in order to attend that meeting. Overseas visits did not charm him anymore. Rather, he found the passport, visa, and customs processes cumbersome. But there was no way out. If you get into the net, you could not escape. Anupam remembered, this was called the 'rat race' in America. He was not at all happy to find that he himself was a big rat running in the race. But as he had already got into the trap, now he had to keep running. In America, the slogan was 'publish or perish'. Academics were perennially running in libraries, laboratories, and archives. Or, they were busy doing fieldwork in bizarre locations. The dormant and withered atmosphere of academia in Bengal, on the other hand, allowed the highly learned professors to indulge in infinite leisure and an utter lack of ambition. They talked big about wisdom, but were actually snooty and envious loudmouths, leading their lives in profound inactivity. Amidst all these, the greed for money or the greed for an award sometimes forced some of them to write books.

Anupam knew that his problem was elsewhere. For him, there was no easy way out. His urge came from within. There was no peace without writing. His competition was not with someone else; it was his future trying to outdo his past. His reputation, forever glowing like the midday sun, must not be allowed to sink. If you wanted to stick to your ideals, you would have to battle every day.

No, it could not go on like this. Not today. He had not written a single sentence yet. Anupam stood up from the typewriter and shifted to the armchair. His work would not progress today. The half-filled glass of whiskey lay on the table, forgotten. Running his fingers over his throat, Anupam tried to feel his voice box. The movement of the vocal chords. No, don't think of those things. Don't think about them. Think of other things. Think of yourself. You can't afford to lose your voice. It is one of the most precious gifts of nature. '*Vachameva prathama*'. Bak is the eighth saint after the *saptarishis**—'*bagastami brahmana samvidana*'—

---

* The *saptarishis* (meaning 'seven sages') are the seven rishis who are extolled at many places in the Vedas and Hindu literature.

she who pronounces the universal utterance, *shabdbrahm*. His power of speech was leaving him. You, Anupam! Have you pondered over the nature of this problem?

'Dadababu?'

'You've come back?' Anupam was hit by the strangeness of his own voice.

'It is late, I guess. It will not be printed this week. It is too late to send it to Delhi and Bombay. They were murmuring something like that. I did not understand everything though. Should I make you some coffee?'

Anupam nodded, forgetting the whiskey.

'Dadababu, shouldn't you call Chorda? You are not keeping well at all.'

'*Ghr … ghr … ghr.*'

'You will not be able to talk like this. Don't refuse. I am calling Chorda. Let him arrange for another doctor today.'

'Ah!' Anupam nodded again in approval. Silently.

Let Niru come with another doctor. Bless you, Keshto.

'Will you have rice for dinner? Ma has made soft rice for you. There won't be any problem in swallowing it. I got some salt water. Can you get up and gargle? You don't have fever, do you?'

Yes, he could. Anupam bobbed his head in affirmation. He did not have fever.

'Get up, then. The water will get cold otherwise.' Anupam straightened up.

'Dadababu,' Keshto asked while handing him the glass of salt water. 'Samirda and his friends did not come any more. Any news....?'

The water in Anupam's mouth turned bitter in a moment.

He spat out the gulp into the basin. Then a smile surfaced on his distinguished face. He jerked his shoulders in assurance. His right hands, holding the glass, swung in the air. His hands almost said, 'Fear not.' Holding the basin with his left hand, he somehow muttered, 'Good....'

Just then, with a loud thud, the bathroom door was shut on Keshto's face.

EIGHTEEN

Nirupam arrived in his rickety Morris Eight by eight in the morning. Ma came with him. Keshto arranged for pen and papers. An emergency appointment with Dr Roychoudhury was fixed.

Dr Roychoudhury repeated exactly what Dr Banerjee had said. He just added that the surgery should be done immediately in Vienna. There was no time to dilly-dally.

Nirupam assured the doctor that it would be done. Then, with a bright smile, he told his brother, 'Dada, don't worry. You will be absolutely fine after getting treated in Vienna.'

Anupam managed to speak a few words after resting at night. He realized that his voice was damaged, particularly because of the twenty cigarettes he had smoked yesterday. No smoking from now on. No matter what people like Ramen did. *'Sammohat smrti-vibhramah smrti-bhramsad buddhi-naso'*—delusion leads to loss of memory, and loss of memory leads to loss of intelligence. 'You went through a state of despair, hypnotized. It is over. Take control of the horses. See that your chariot does not lose its way.'

Ma had to go back with Niru, as his son had exams. Nowadays, sitting for exams was another exam itself.

Nirupam dropped his brother along with a bagful of the medicines, injection ampules, capsules, etc. On the way back, he also spoke to a compounder in the nearest dispensary who would come regularly for the injections. Nirupam was as organized as Anupam, but their worlds were different. Before leaving, Ma left a string of advices for Keshto, 'Keep a slate and chalk handy. Anu should not talk at all. Don't let him receive phone calls. I will stay here from Friday after Khoka finishes his exams. Till then, please see that my Anu does not talk, dear.'

Anupam had always been a man of few words. If he spoke less, it would not be something out of the way. He found a bunch of letters on the table after reaching home.

There was an invitation for a book fair. A student's wedding. An evening of American folk music. A senior British writer's speech at the British Council. An invitation from the Osmania University to deliver a series of lectures. Osmania? In Hyderabad? No, he could not go there. Not near Sudha. Another invitation was for delivering the inaugural lecture in a training camp on journalism. This was a fortnightly affair in Srinagar.

All invitations were for delivering speeches and lectures.

But his voice? His left hand went up to his throat. The latter surrendered itself to the gentle caress of the palm. What would happen to the lecture invitations now?

He did not open the green envelope. Menaka's letter was shredded to pieces and went right into the dustbin. He won't be receiving letters in brown envelopes for the time being. Maybe, six months later. Maybe, when Sudha would feel like it again. She could send six pages from her diary. Or—Anupam's eyelids trembled slightly as he thought about her—who knows, she might not feel like writing again, whimsical as she was.

There was no need to think about letters now. The present concern was speech. Bringing it back. What if his voice did not come back? What if?

So many invitations, such popularity, warmth, worldwide fame, a series of romantic affairs—how much of it would he sustain if his voice disappeared?

The nation was used to listening to his voice every week. 'Roy's Corner' had earned massive popularity as a national programme on radio; it was considered a valuable analysis of world politics. This was new. It had been going on air for two years now. This would also have to stop now.

His tryst with Bangalore–Mysore–Chandigarh–Chittor would end forever. Should I go to Prague or should I go to Jakarta? He wouldn't need to face such difficult questions any more. Maybe, it was not that bad?

Anupam pushed the rest of the letters aside. He went to the bathroom, latched it, and then stood before the mirror. He tried to see his face in the shadowy light. Was it visible? Even though it was daytime, the room was laden with darkness. He liked the quietness around, but definitely not the darkness.

The mirror continued to look blurred even when he switched on the light. He wiped it carefully with the corner of his towel. Then he opened his lips slightly and bent down on his reflection, almost in the manner of a kiss. The vapour from his breath spread on the mirror, enshrouding his reflection. He wiped it again. This time he used the other corner of the towel. It was as if he was wiping the fatigue of lovemaking off a love-struck princess with a muslin kerchief. Now it was quite clear. It would possibly not get better than this.

Like a gymnast, Anupam held the basin with both his hands and moved as close to the mirror as possible. He could see the visage of a worried and tired middle-aged man in the mirror. His forehead had furrows. The frames of his thick glasses made his eyes look enormous and shiny like an octopus', and incisive like a snake's. His eyebrows were uneven. He was known to be a handsome man. But how? He removed his glasses. His eyes were lost somewhere, missing even from his reflection.

He took out his handkerchief and rubbed the lenses. His eyes looked terribly huge once he wore them.

Was he handsome? How? Complexion? It was rather on the darker side. Built? Medium. His frame was tallish, but he was not very tall. Quite like a betel nut tree. Balance was the key. His physique was balanced exactly like his behaviour. He looked taller because his lower half was taller than his upper half. Was it the same with his behaviour? Lost in thoughts, he removed his shirt. The small mirror in the bathroom could accommodate his reflection up till his bust; nothing beyond that. A hint of hairy chest was visible through his vest, with proud shoulders and strong arms. His fit body has been approved by the government health department's seal. There was no dearth of seductiveness! There was no stamp of intellect showing through the sensuality of his summer cool vest. No drudgery or anxiety. There was just an unquestioned sense of power.

He analysed his face next. An oval-shaped face with a pointed chin. His nose was thick, broad, and fleshy. There were creases on both sides of his nose. He tried to emulate a smile by shifting his moustache. The creases deepened. He examined his teeth, as they do in the toothpaste ads. Yellowish and uneven. His laughter had ceased to be natural since he was fourteen, when the left canine had to be cast in gold. He opened his mouth and saw nicotine stains on his teeth. He twisted his tongue. Voice box, the goddess of speech. The tongue was blue underneath; the veins were showing. This shade of blue can be seen in cows' tongues. There was a cowshed in Roy Mansion. As a child, Niru used to spend a lot of time there feeding the cows. A boy called Anu would climb the guava tree there to watch it.

His cheeks were sunken. There were a few spots of white on the greenish shadow of his stubble. Strange! Did he forget to shave while hurrying to meet the doctor in the morning? Anupam! Have you started making mistakes in your daily chores? For a trivial reason? Now, he checked his skin. Dark patches under his spectacles. There were pimple marks and freckles. He looked at his hair. A shock of hair on his eyebrows. Though he could not see it in the mirror, he knew his hair was thinning slowly. Strands of hair came off in the hairbrush every day. Some of them were grey.

No, there was nothing special. Nothing but that pair of huge and sharp preying eyes. Instead of drawing people close, his eyes pushed them away.

He tried to pull the skin beneath his chin with his thumb and forefinger. It slipped away. There was a strange sense of relief. Good. The sun had not set yet.

This time he had been challenged by nature herself. Never before in his life had his peace and quiet been hampered like this. So far he knew that any kind of battle could be conquered with intelligence. But was this an impossible task? Ever since his adolescence, Anupam's work was to defeat the laws of nature.

Earlier, it was only about enjoyment, but the current issue was different. Basic and gross—straightforward.

This time, the issue involved the presence or absence of one of his sense organs.

Anupam, pay no heed. It is not acceptable to give so much time to something as petty as your body. But what was the way out? He suddenly felt insignificant, like the tiny Gulliver in the fist of the giant Brobdingnag. So long he was the lord of all his senses. His fleshly desires were suddenly overpowering him and encroaching upon his world. They were claiming something as precious as Ekalavya's thumb—the voice of Anupam Roy, the orator. He realized that intelligence would not shield him in this battle. 'But intelligence is a weapon, Anupam,' the voice within him said. 'Try. Even if you lose your voice forever, your world is not going to end, right?'

You could determine someone's civility by one's use of words. It was through the web of words that you could manage to gauge the decency of a person.

Anupam, you are not the undying sculpture crafted on a temple wall. You are not Rama, the one who speaks only through His eyes, or a well-structured lump of flesh without brains.

What magic did this tired, shrewd, nondescript, matured man spell? What if this experienced, prudent face lost its voice ... ?

Numerous female admirers in the elite quarters of London were charmed by Dr Johnson's words, a poor, plain-looking man. Yours will desert you! Anupam, where would your Ruma–Nalini–Menaka–Kamalkali be then? Would Sir Raghavan, Krishnamurthy, Mohan Rao, and others light up your life even then? Where would you find your dear students who pass out and add to your fan following every year? And what about those people who have never seen you, whom you have never seen, but are fans just because of the magic of your voice on Akashbani? What magic have you seen on that silent face? What magic? What have you found in it?

Anupam switched off the light. The midday sunshine vanished from the room, leaving it motionlessly dark. Running his fingers through his hair, Anupam tried to contemplate whether a voiceless life would be as dark as this room. Human voice was like a burning lamp; it brought the mind's treasures to light. A lot like this lamp. The mirror reflected his charisma when the light was on.

The moment the light was switched off, the mirror turned dim. Even the blue tiles and the white basin were not visible now. Anupam's reflection ...

How much of his life and personality would go away with his voice, if it went, that is? How much of him would vanish from the public eye?

He could see a tongueless man's living head buried upto his neck in an endless, sunburnt, empty desert. There were just the two helpless, spherical eyeballs moving restlessly. The last sign of life.

Shuddered, Anupam rushed out of the dark bathroom. His eyes were burning as he came into the broad daylight. Anupam thought,

Voice—a great wonder, joy.

Voice—a magic web.

Voice—a special treasure.

Did I not recognize its wealth so long just because it was effortless and unearned? Or was it because I had never been scared of losing it?

Humans have natural resources other than intelligence. We get to appreciate their importance only when nature wants to snatch it away from us.

Anupam tried to understand whether he should have been more grateful for this wealth. Something must have gone wrong. But what could have gone wrong? What mistake? What gratitude? 'Gratitude' was a rather wrong word. The actual word here was 'lesson'. This experience would be a lesson for him. A new lesson—life was full of such surprises.

Anupam cooled down and started working on the subcommittee's oil report. He had had enough of worldly attraction ... enough of destructive thoughts. Now, some serious work would get done.

NINETEEN

'Don't worry about Vienna, Dada. Everything will be arranged. We just need to inform Jethima,' Niru said.

'Don't you dare, Niru! Do not tell Jethima,' Anupam roared in his husky, yet hoarse voice. He was surprised at himself. Niru was stunned, but kept calm.

'I was thinking of borrowing the money from her. Jethima lends money to so many people with interest. Leave it. I will not tell her. I have lots of other sources.'

Dr Roychoudhury had pressed for the surgery to be done by the next month. His throat condition should not be allowed to fester. He had been insisting Anupam not to wait for long with this constant irritation. Other kind of complications might develop. But covering such large expenses was a problem. Where would they get the money so soon? Dr Banerjee and Dr Roychoudhury wanted to start contacting the doctors in Vienna and discuss the plan of action as soon as possible.

Anupam Roy is not poor. Apart from his regular salary, his books earn him good profit. However, he was currently short of cash, as all his money has been spent in booking a flat in Camac Street. The construction of the flat was almost over. All of his savings had been invested there.

From Roy Mansion in Darjipara to Camelia Apartments in Camac Street, Anupam had travelled an endless path.

The middle-class values of Darjipara had given way to an elite sensibility in Anupam. He hardly looked at the right side of the menu card while ordering food at restaurants. Taking a taxi did not mean a breathless rush. He could ask his friend's wife to make him a cup of tea with the taxi waiting. There was one discrepancy though; his Marxist ideals were becoming stronger as the 'quality' of his life was getting better and better. This was not logical. Anupam genuinely believed in equality. It was not limited to arguing in public or on pen and paper.

The next evening, Nirupam entered Anupam's flat triumphantly and called out, 'Keshto, make me a strong cup of coffee. Or does Dada want to celebrate with something else? Given that Ma is not here today. Good. Everything has been arranged. Just the passage needs to be booked now. We need the permission from Reserve Bank.'

'Everything has been arranged? How did you do it? Who gave you the money? From where did you borrow it? The bank?'

'Please do not talk so much, Dada. Keshto, where is the slate? Who needs to give, Dada? The money was there. I have given an application to withdraw my provident fund. Bithi's unit trust policy has also been arranged to be sold. Everything has been completed; they just need to be finalized. No Boroma, nothing. Everything has been done in a straightforward, official manner. Keshto, leave the coffee. Get some soda and ice. Dada, bring out the drinks. Let's!'

'Niru … ' Anupam's lament seemed to come out not from his throat, but from a secret well of blood hidden beneath his ribs.

'What have you done, Niru?'

He realized that he was pressing his brother's hands. Anupam let go. 'Have you gone mad?' he asked roughly.

'Ah, Dada. Please use the slate. Don't you remember?'

'Are you crazy, Niru! Bithi's money?'

'I think you have gone mad. People save money for emergencies. Bithi's money is your money too.'

'What if you people get into … ?'

Niru's laughter echoed through Anupam's tiny flat.

'This is why Khana* had said that teachers are not intelligent. Arré, you are always there if we land up in some trouble.'

'Listen, Niru. I have money.'

Anupam could faintly hear an unknown, feeble voice speaking with intense earnestness, 'Niru, do not ever spend that money. I have money.'

It was Nirupam's turn to be surprised. 'Is it? Do you have money? Where is it?'

* Khana was a woman poet and soothsayer believed to have lived in twelfth-century Bengal.

Anupam replied in his croaky voice, 'I do not have the money right now, but can get it the moment I want. I have been refusing an offer for five years. I will take it up now.'

'If you could take it up, why didn't you for so long? What offer is it? And who made it?'

'The reasons are trivial. It is an offer from the *Daily Star*. They want me to be their editor.'

Consoling himself, Anupam said, 'I have to give up teaching.' Then he carefully touched his throat, 'I have to change my profession, anyway.'

Niru was bemused. His brother had to change his profession in order to arrange for the money? Did he think over the whole issue properly? Anupam confirmed that it was indeed so. Dada's decision was judicious as always, and had to be accepted. Niru agreed to it.

After chalking out the whole plan, Nirupam left. Anupam tried to recollect Niru's childhood Anupam used to be very naughty. He would get into brawls with the boys in Darjipara regularly. The practice of vegetarian diet did not help in keeping his sensibilities non-violent. On the other hand, Niru would burst into tears on seeing a broken nest with broken eggs. Anupam never got into fights; neither did he get dirty cats or flea-infested dogs home, as his brother did. Niru had always been different. 'Crazy boy,' Anupam smiled to himself affectionately. Should he call Ramsharan Agarwal to Delhi once? Or should he go via Mangeshkar? No, he should not do that. If he accepted the offer, his position would be way above Mangeshkar. He had to approach Ramsharanji, or else Sir Raghavan, the head of the concern.

Anupam remembered that Raghavan was in Calcutta yesterday. If he called Mangeshkar, he would be able to say where Raghavan was now.

No, let it be. Let this wait for a while now.

A tiny speck of the sky could be seen from between the curtains. There were three shining stars adjacent to each other. Binu jhi had said, 'They are Rama-Lakshman-Sita.' But their father told them that it was a constellation, the Belt of Orion—it was now chained to Anupam's window. Huh!

Krishnachaitanya would sleep on a mat in the terrace on summer evenings. He called all the children up there and familiarized them with the stars and constellations. He introduced them to the universe through slokas and stories. He was the one to teach Anupam the names of constellations and the addresses of planets. You feel a bit uneasy when you look at billions of stars while lying on your back—an enormous, unknown land of mystery. But all the stars seemed so close in his childhood, as accessible as lights in the neighbours' windows.

He used to like Krishnachaitanya Roy in those times, until Fulkaki …

Anupam tried to focus on things. He needed to call up Mangeshkar and get in touch with Raghavan Sir.

Look at the watch. It will be soon past the proper time to call people up. Do not delay, Anupam.

His hands were not functioning. It was almost eleven then. Not a good time to call anyone. Tomorrow? Call them tomorrow. It would not be difficult to get through Raghavan Sir, wherever he might be, in Delhi or Bombay. The only problem was with the editorial policy. The general guidelines of *Daily Star* did not match Anupam's ideology. He could not take up the editorship unless the editorial policy was in his hands. Would Sir Raghavan agree? His own paper would not run on his own ideas. Nobody would stand that, especially when they had a pronounced editorial policy. He was not like Mr Dastur. He was an orthodox Tamilian Brahmin, that too one who had earned knighthood.

He would be no less obstinate in his views than you, Anupam! Besides, this would not be a freelance position; this would be a job. True, he has a lot of respect for you, Anupam. Yet, will you be able to persuade him? Can you, Anupam?

Anupam rummaged through the cupboards to look for some leftover tobacco, an old box maybe, but as he was searching, he remembered the doctor's warning—he was not supposed to have it. Closing the cupboard, he went out to the verandah. A rickshaw made its way through the street. It was followed by a pack of dogs. There was a middle-aged inebriated man on the rickshaw. 'You are happy,' Anupam told the man. 'You are a free man, beyond sorrow, happiness, or fear.'

Anupam looked beyond the roads, far away. The red light on the terrace of the skyscraper flickered throughout the night, as if alerting the sky of the limits of the earth.

The still earth beneath was marking the limits of the noisy speed piercing the sky above. It was saying, 'Do not stoop low, you will perish. Fly higher, fly even higher. Your way is blocked here, because your sky ends here.'

Anupam looked higher. This time, not only the belt of big stars, but the entire constellation of Orion was clear in the sky. His instructions were different for celestial beings, showing them a different horizon. 'Do not go higher. This is the cosmos—the sky is beyond the sky. This light is the light from distant planets. You have no right to this fiery bunch of stars.'

What time is it?

First thing, tomorrow morning, he would have to call Mangeshkar. There would be two conditions: one, Ramsharanji and Sir Raghavan would not interfere regarding the editorial policy; two, Anupam should have full rights to write elsewhere as well. What would he tell Dastur otherwise?

He could also borrow thirty thousand rupees without taking any of these steps. He could pay back the loan in installments after recovering. What if they said no? That was more likely. He would have to think of an alternative. Taking a loan from a bank should not be that difficult. *What ails thou, Faustus*? If there was no chance of getting sleep, he might as well complete the report of the oil subcommittee now.

'You will work at this time of the night?' Anupam was startled at Keshto's remark.

‘Keshto, you didn’t sleep?’ Anupam’s lips moved voicelessly.

‘You did not have dinner tonight.’

‘No appetite. Have you not eaten either? Goodness!’

‘Me? I had my dinner long back. Go to sleep, Dadababu. You are not keeping well.’

‘Let me write this.’

‘It is two.’

‘No, it is one-thirty.’

‘It is all the same.’

‘I have to write something important.’

‘Let it be. Go to sleep. You have taken an injection. Do not type today.’

(Don’t bother me, Keshto.)

‘You sleep, Keshto.’

‘Will you not sleep?’

‘After a while.’

Keshto left the room.

Keshto, you don’t know. I can’t fall asleep. I am awake not because I have work; I am working because I am awake. I know you are with me always. You have always been a well-wisher. I still can’t tell you why I am not getting sleep.

At last, his head felt heavy. It was like a few lead-filled spheres were rolling inside his skull. The Orion had disappeared, treading into the darkness; the chariot of another brilliant being had appeared in the east in its divine glory.

Did the writing come out well? It was impossible to think about anything at this moment. Crash cymbals were echoing in his head, and a deep curtain screen of fatigue was descending on his eyes and mind. It was about to be morning soon. He needed to make that call now.

No, not yet. It is only four-thirty now. You could not call someone before eight.

He dragged himself towards the bed. He should have taken a sleeping pill at night. He forgot, strangely. It would not work now. He would go off schedule if he took the medicine and went to sleep now. He would rather go for a walk. But he was feeling unwell ... the red light in the multi-storeyed building was still throbbing inside him; it was going to tear apart his nerves.

Getting up from his bed, Anupam went to the bathroom. As he turned on the shower, the cool beads of water drenched his naked body. The water caressed and consoled his nerves.

His father possessed a book on natural remedies. According to that, the treatment for every illness is bathing in the river twice a day. Arthritis, dysentery, cold and cough—bath. The remedy for sleeplessness should also be the same.

But this was not a dip in the river; it was taking a shower under a flowing stream of water. This was another natural remedy. It, too, cooled the nerves. It balanced the blood pressure. Even in the West, standing in the shower is supposed to be the primary cure for all nerve-related diseases. *Dharapat*, or cascade, as it is called in Bengali. Surprisingly, this is what the Bengali primers of multiplication tables are called. 'Why does a book on multiplication tables have such a poetic title?' Anupam had asked his father as a child.

Dharapat? His father replied that in ancient times, the saints were mathematicians as well as poets. Such titles descend from the Indian tradition. Take the word for Bengali alphabet, *barnomala* or a 'string of letters'. Compared to a harsh word like 'alphabet', it is much more musical and colourful. His father would wander away while talking about mundane things. He belonged to a different world. But that was not his actual identity. That was the mask he wore in front of his sons. Just like his daily bath in the Ganga. For him, taking a dip meant a dip in the Ganga. The current must be flowing. He recited the Ganga *stotra** every time he bathed, even at home. O, Goddess Ganga, can you truly save the three worlds? Can your waves really cool down the heated sorrows? Can you stitch back a fragmented world with your affection?

Breaking the sound of water, a bell rang somewhere. Was it an early morning knock? 'No, not on my door. May be on the next-door neighbour's flat.' The bell got shriller. It was just five. Who could it be? A telegram? May be for the flat next door. Anupam turned off the tap and strained his ears. Keshto was opening the door. 'Then it must be my house!'

* *Stotra* is a Sanskrit word meaning ode, eulogy, or a hymn of praise.

The soap case fell as he tried to wrap the towel around his body. The soap jumped out like a frog. Though aware that it was not alive, Anupam took two steps back in an act of self-defence. He picked up the soap, washed it in the tap water, and put it back in the case.

Everything remained as it was. Only the wet soap was dimpled due to the fall. Anupam did not notice.

Who rang the bell?

Because he surrendered their kitbag? Somen's body was found near Ganga the day before yesterday….

Anupam suddenly felt that he was yet to know two-thirds of the four parts of life. What did he learn by working so long? What did he gain? What was the truth? What did you do to reach the truth? On which side was the true face of life covered with a golden vessel? Was it focused on Anupam or Sudha?

Let it be. He could not take it anymore. Let the boys come. He would face them and ask, 'What has happened? What is the issue? So early in the morning?'

Anupam came out. His shirt was wet and his waist covered by a large towel. With slippers and glasses on, he came out wiping his head with a smaller towel. No matter how early or how hot it was, Anupam never came out in public without being properly dressed or without his glasses or slippers.

'What is it, Keshto? So early in the morning?' Anupam tried to ask, but the words jumbled. His voice had worsened as he stayed up all night.

'Dadababu, Ma has come.'

Anupam was relieved. So it was raining flowers in the battlefield instead of raining arrows! But why is Ma here so early? Has something happened to Niru....?

'Why are you bathing so early in the morning? Did you not sleep at night?'

Anupam was happy to hear his mother's normal tone. But his curiosity doubled.

'Keshto, make some tea for Dadababu and Chorda. I pulled Niru out of the bed. Anu, how is your voice now?'

Did she just come for this? So early? She could have enquired about his health on the phone. But all he could say was, '*Ghargharghr*.'

'O, God! What a terrible state! Come to the room, I have to tell you something.'

Nirupam added, 'Dada, Ma has a request. You change into pyjamas first. Then we can talk.'

Ma said, 'Anu dear, have you already informed the owners of the other newspaper house?'

'What do you mean?'

'Niru told me that you have a plush job offer in hand for the last five years, but you have not accepted it yet.'

'Hmm.'

'Don't accept that offer.'

'Ma?'

'Yes, my son. I am your mother and I am asking you not to take up that job. Your father would have said the same thing had he been alive.'

'Ma!'

'I thought about it, Anu. I have come very early in the morning and dragged Niru along just to say this. How can these things be discussed over telephone? You should never do something that goes against your heart.'

'But ... ?'

'No more questions. Your heart is not in that job. No, you do not have to take it up.'

'But Ma!' (Why are you asking me not to take it?)

'I am not educated. I cannot tell the good from the bad. But you are educated; you know the pros and cons. That is why I am asking you not to take it up. When you have sensed something unacceptable about it since the last five years, there must be something wrong in it. Do not take up that job.'

'But now ... '

'Even great men take wrong decisions when they fall into trouble. You have a brother. Your mother is still alive. Why should you do something against your will? You have sufficient resources.'

'Dada, did you call up Raghavan?'

'Could not call yesterday.'

'God has been kind. Radhamadhav has saved us. Do not call them, Anu. Don't worry about money. I have kept some jewellery for your wife. We can mortgage that and get some money. Niru will arrange for the rest in some way.'

Mortgage? The idea struck him like a flash of lightning. His flat could be kept under mortgage too. He could also do without the flat. He would get the entire money back. There won't be any dearth of customers for that posh flat in Camac Street. A lot of people would line up to own a rich apartment in this poor country.

If the issue could be resolved by giving up the flat, then it was not necessary to take such pains.

Are you so money-minded? Anupam, you desire these things so much that you were about to take up that offer by *Daily Star*. You consider yourself ascetic, indifferent, dispassionate, neutral, and calm. Is that all false? Why didn't it strike you that you even have a provident fund?

You earn much more than that Niru. But Niru is still richer!

Niru's treasures are infinite. Niru, a chatty, soppy, light-hearted family man, was ready to shower all his savings on someone so easily!

'Ma, I will sell off the flat. I will get some liquid money from that. All my money is stuck here. Do not worry, Niru.'

A sharp pang of pain escaped Anupam's throat. The moment he said this, the throbbing red light on the skyscraper inside his head went off. Even the drone inside his ears became silent.

Gradually, Anupam's mind was carpeted with the early morning stillness, the calmness of the dawn, and the chirping of birds.

'Good, now I can go to office in peace,' Niru said after finishing his tea and biscuits. 'Dada, really! It did not strike us about giving up the flat, neither me nor you.'

Ma said, 'Leave it. Good that he thought about it now. Niru, I have asked your wife to do the puja. I will stay with Anu today.'

TWENTY

Anupam started to feel drowsy as he heard Niru's car leaving. He suddenly felt very tired after keeping awake the entire night. He told his mother that he would not have breakfast and would like to sleep.

He felt so relieved lying on the bed. A crisp morning with blossoming light and birds' songs filled his mind. He would not have to call Mangeshkar anymore. He would rather meet Sukumar Chakraborty once regarding the flat. One victory, one decision had been taken. But imagining how Sukumar Chakraborty's face would look when Anupam would return the flat seemed to prick his brain with a thousand pins.

'Many people return the flats. They cannot afford it at the last moment,' Sukumar said this very often. Anupam was a part of that troop now.

Just then, someone's slender fingers ran through his hair. Fulkaki! The thought triggered a sense of pain. The same old sense of claustrophobia. As if Anupam was allergic to this word—*Anu's Fulkaki. Fulkaki's Anu*. Fulkaki used to put him to sleep, just like this, by running her soft, thin fingers through his hair. That boy, named Anu, was the centre of attention for days and nights to Fulkaki, his lonely child-widow aunt.

Rubbish thoughts. There was no use thinking of her again. Fulkaki was long dead.

'Did you say something, Anu?' Anupam was surprised to hear his mother's voice.

'Nothing!'

'I thought you said something. Are you okay? Should I massage your head?'

'No, Ma. I am feeling sleepy.'

'Sleep, my dear. Sleep. Let me stroke your hair.'

'Ma!' Anupam called out to his mother after being restless for some time. He was not used to being tended by his mother. Theirs was a joint family. When they were kids, his mother never took out time separately for her children, unless they were sick. That too, after Fulkaki passed away.

Today, suddenly, at this age, he felt more uneasy than happy to receive his mother's touch. 'Ma, remove your hand. I cannot take your caress.' But he could not bring himself to say it to her.

'Ma?'

'Yes?'

'Why did you and Grandma give so much indulgence to Baba? How could you do so?'

His mother's fingers froze inside his hair. As if someone was playing 'statue' with Ma.

'Who are you talking about, Anu?'

A shriek of pain tore through her voice.

'About Baba,' Anupam sounded tired but composed. 'Why were you so lenient towards that man?'

'Lenient?'

'You women are very cruel. You have no feelings for other women. How did you tolerate the man for whom Fulkakima had to die?'

'But what did Baba have to do with that? Fulkaki did not die because of your father.'

Ma's quiet reply ran smooth and fast as a train whistling past a station full of distracted, bewildered passengers.

'Ma....'

Anupam's refined voice had nowadays become even softer due to his illness. But, at this moment, no one would believe how shrill and loud he sounded. His mother was shocked, but remained quiet.

'Ma?' Anupam went back to the decent and humble notch.

'Yes, dear.'

The boy who had seen a deformed, burnt dead body one fine morning in the courtyard thirty years ago said, 'Are you sure, Ma?'

'What should I be unsure about?'

'Then why did Jethima say those things to Baba?'

'Don't pay heed to what your jethima said....'

'Why? Why should not I?'

'Your jethima did not know anything, son.'

'Then why didn't you protest, Ma? She says the same thing till date....'

'Didi does not know anything.'

'Why? Why doesn't she know? Why didn't you tell her that my father is not a criminal, a murderer, and a person of loose morals ... maybe, my father was none of what she said?'

'What maybe? He was not any of these. He was a godly person,' his mother touched her forehead in reverence.

'Be quiet, Ma.'

'Anu, did you not realize how much he loved you?'

'Ma, why didn't you tell me then?'

'What could I have said?'

'Why didn't you say that Jethima was lying, that she was wrong?'

'How could I? Your father did not let me say anything.'

'He did not let you say? Why? Why?' (Whom was he trying to save? Whose follies were he trying to cover up?)

'Anu, you are talking too much. You should not talk at all.'

'Let me speak. Why didn't he allow it? Whose mistakes were he trying to hide?'

'I cannot blame you. Even your grandmother could not stand it anymore. Your father forced her to be silent about it.'

Anupam's cousin's sister-in-law had asked Binu jhi, their old maidservant, 'Is it true that Boudi's uncle burnt this family's youngest son's wife to death?'

'Are you crazy?' Binu jhi retorted. 'She immolated herself.'

The sister-in-law continued, 'But the child in her womb was actually Boudi's uncle's....'

Binu jhi said, 'That's what Boroma says, but I do not believe that. Must be someone else. Chotobabu is like God!'

'Or a pseudo-God. Hypocrite, murderer, promiscuous. He should be hung to death!'

'Baba made her promise? Not to reveal the truth? Why, Ma?'

His mother's voice softened as she responded to her son's questions. Her fingers started stroking Anupam's hair again. She continued in a dreamy tone.

'Your father did not allow it, Anu. He kept saying that disclosing the truth would not help. Fulbou would not come back. God will look after her. Please give some respite to the person who is still alive. Boudi should not know the truth.

'Even I felt restless like you. He said, "No one should bring it up. If Dada has told this version to Boudi in fear, then let Boudi believe that." He went and told your grandmother, "Ma, you know that I am not at fault. Anu's mother knows the same and, of course, Dada knows about it. *Byas*, the problem is solved. I do not have to answer to anyone else. It will not harm if Boudi does not know the truth. Let there be peace between Dada and her."

'I could not say a word about this because of your father. Even the servants knew about it. Your father called them and had to coax and bribe them so that they would not open their mouths. Dada had seven daughters. Only two of them were married by then. The news could brew trouble if it came out.'

'How terrible! Why didn't you tell me, Ma? Why? Why? Why did you never bring this up?'

Anupam groaned. Muffled screams escaped his lips. Lying on his belly in his usual way, he kept clawing at the pillow.

'What could I have said, Anu? You never asked. I told you the truth today because you asked.'

'Niru? Niru knows?'

'Yes. He got to know about it long back. Your father told him about the incident.'

'He told Niru himself?' Anupam sounded crestfallen.

'Yes. He asked your father about the incident after his matriculate exams were over, "Baba, is it true what Jethima says about Fulkaki? I want to know the truth."

'Baba took Niru to the family temple, told him the truth, and made him promise in front of Radhamadhav that he would never talk about the incident.

'You never asked about it. I thought you knew. You were slightly older than Niru at that time.'

Anupam could hear the music of the spheres. That divine music in the orbit which only angels could hear. Anupam's inner world was filled with those extrasensory notes.

For a moment.

He then recollected that grey, icy, and windy afternoon in London—the alien streets laden with mud and snow. He buried his face deeper in the pillow. It was like he could bury his memories like that, his errors and his sins ... yes, his sins.

Anupam clenched his teeth, opened his mouth twice, and let out a suppressed, silent, private, desolate sound, 'Ba ba.'

TWENTY-ONE

'My eyes are closed, but not my mind.'

'Yato yato niscarati manas cancalam asthiram.'

Get your mind back, bring it under your control. Anupam, compose yourself. You could not do it. Admit it, you could not. You are confused, you are proud, Anupam. You are greedy, you are lustful, and you get easily angered. You are unforgiving, admit it. Anupam, you are impure. The period of mourning will be endless. You will never be happy, never be at peace.

In that bone-chilling, reckless, foreign wind, you have lost your right to pay homage to your father. Recall, try to recall, Anupam. Do not deny your memory. Memory is truth, and truth begets freedom.

You rejoiced at the news of your father's death, celebrated it in the wildest manner possible, and cried profusely (for Fulkaki) in the arms of poor and innocent Maria. Was it grief? Or your desire? It was like a celebration followed by another, another bout of sins—a deeper one. You addressed Maria, the woman in your bed, as Fulkaki throughout the night. There is no limit to your sins. No forgiveness for you. Listen, Maria, I am a sinner.

'Pap'ham, papkarma'ham, papatma, paapsambhav ...'

'Baba, listen, there is no end to my sins.'

Today, suddenly, the thoughts of Maria started shaking the roots of Anupam's memory. Toxic flowers fell from its branches. Anupam found the fragrance obnoxious. The flowers of memory encroached and slowly enveloped all of Anupam's present.

When he disembarked on a foreign shore, he never felt that he would face any trouble. He found a room at Maria's place. The landladies during those times were very particular about the tenant's race. There were endless fights and distinctions between white, brown, and black tenants. Maria was a white woman, but of central European Jewish descent. She herself was a foreigner in the UK. Perhaps, that was the reason she rented out her place to brown-skinned people. Anupam was very young, just stepping into his manhood. Maria, on the other hand, was in the peak of her youth. Maria was pretty and quite well-off; she was into the business of hat-making. She had been married once, but divorced long back. She was a caring hostess to the foreign students who stayed at her place. Anupam took Maria's shelter.

He experienced something completely new. It was something which never crossed his mind in his own country. Something which never struck him when he was floating in the endless blue waters during his tedious voyage. That terrible, formless, unquenchable emptiness took charge of him in the busy, crowded city of London.

After the initial excitement of staying overseas and free from the regimented life of Roy Mansion got over, he kept longing to see a Bengali face or hear someone speak in Bengali. But his experience suggested him a different direction. You could never tie a bunch of hearts without stalks. You needed something to hold the hearts together.

Loneliness can only be overcome by a sense of attachment. Anupam could never think of being possessive about a person. That was the first time his heart craved for having a woman in life. Then in his body, and in his brains. What started off as a helpless seeking emotional shelter went on to become a conscious form of emotional exploitation. Earlier, he would pray for her love; eventually, he played the role of a seasoned lover.

Being with Maria did not just mean wining, dining, movies, and theatres; soon, everything from his ties, handkerchief, to shirts and shoes was taken care of. She did not let him have any worries, neither financial nor domestic.

Anupam found a lot of time to concentrate on his studies after he found a stable and safe shelter in Maria. He got back his confidence, composure, and emotional security in the warmth of her company. In Maria, he found a home away from home, a country outside his own.

With time, their relationship came to an assumed edge. Both of them wondered about the social consequences of their togetherness. There was a ray of hope on one of their minds and shades of anxiety on the other.

The young Anupam had come of age in those two years, and Maria's shining youth was slowly leaning towards the horizon. She had started to type his thesis for him. Typing theses was a part-time job for her, but it was not a job when it came to Anupam. Her endless favours kept entwining him. Anupam was feeling stifled liked a caged animal and was dying to get out.

Anupam realized that a middle-aged, full-bodied, Jewish woman's stiletto heels would never enter the pious Roy Mansion's vegetarian kitchen. Even if it works out with his family by some magic, it would never work in Anupam's life. Maria, I won't be able to live at your mercy. His life could not be controlled by someone else's will.

Maria, you have helped me so much that I cannot tolerate you. Your heart has been the witness to the most vulnerable moments of my life. That heart of yours, I cannot carry with me.

Freedom chanced upon him soon. Niru fell in love with a girl from the neighbourhood, married her, and wrote a note of apology to his brother. About two years after Baba's death. Niru had just started to work after finishing college. Along with the letter, he sent his newly-wed bride's photograph, her love glittering through her nose ring and her eyes speaking volumes of happiness. Bithi's photograph sent Anupam a brainwave. This could be his ticket to freedom. It had been four years since he was abroad. He would return to India soon. The first draft of his thesis had already been typed. The final version had to be typed out somewhere else anyway.

Anupam thought of giving it a try, come what may.

Maria tidied his desk every day. She used to stack all the Bengali letters carefully on one side.

Anupam started writing an airmail letter—the letter which was never to be finished.

The letter had just an address and date written on the right and 'Darling' scribbled on the left. It was folded, with Bithi's photograph slipped inside. Anupam tucked it under a few books with meticulous carelessness, so that it could be noticed.

After arranging this, Anupam left for the day, his destination being The India Office Library.

Things worked out just as he had expected. He came home and found Maria crying profusely. Her face was red and swollen. She did not let him enter her room, threw out Anupam's books, clothes, shoes one by one outside, and kept crying out, 'I should have known it. All Indians are cheats and liars....'

Anupam pretended to be guilty and did really well in his role. He did not try to pacify her. Who knows, she might forgive him! Maria was madly in love with him. Kneeling down before him, she shook Anupam's shoulders vigorously, 'Why didn't you tell me you had a wife at home? Why didn't you? Why? Why? Why?' Anupam was picking up his clothes, books, copies, and shoes scattered on the floor and neatly arranging them in his suitcase. He kept saying in a calm and decent tone, 'Let me explain, darling. Listen to me, sweetheart. Please listen.'

But Anupam did not try to explain anything. Nor did he address the charges Maria levelled against him in a fit of frenzy. Rather, he said, 'Good. If you do not want to listen to me, I will not say it. I am leaving. Darling, I will never disturb you again. Thanks a lot. Look after yourself.' He departed from the house like a rejected, hurt lover. Then he landed up in Jeff's house with his belongings. Everyone got to know that Maria picked up a petty fight and evicted Roy out of her house. That too, at a crucial juncture, when he was about to complete his thesis. A wave of sympathy swept through his friends. Both the Indians and the British agreed that the Jews were a community of mean people. It was also discussed that though Hitler's method was defective, he was not actually 'wrong'. Anupam had observed that irrespective of being white- or brown-skinned, people just needed an excuse to mudsling the Jews. Maria Epstein got splattered in that mud.

He never blamed himself for this; his conscience remained untarnished. Why did Maria have to be so predictable? Who would protect such stupid, emotional people from devastation?

Maria, foolish Maria, didn't you understand that this was actually good for you? There was no loss of face for you. Instead of letting you play the part of the rejected woman, I let you play the woman who had the guts to reject someone. You should look at the incident as a positive one. Wouldn't you call it an act of consideration?

Anupam was considerate indeed. Let us recall the case of Nalini Deshpande. Standing in front of an open window in a multi-storeyed hotel in Bombay, Nalini told him, 'Anupam, I am going to jump right now.' Anupam looked at the queen's necklace and wished, 'Please do.' But what he said was entirely different. He knelt down before the lady and said, 'Nalini, listen. I do not deserve you. Think about your children. If you weigh them against me, I am so trivial, so irrelevant. Your life is extremely valuable. Nalini, remember your children's faces. Am I that worthy? Many Anupams will come and go.' A frenzied, tear-drenched Nalini hit Anupam with weak, shaky hands. A feeble slap landed on Anupam's precious cheeks. He felt a surge of anger within him, but said in a gentle, honeyed tone, 'Hit me as much as you want, but just think of Pappu and Guddi!' Nalini broke down. Anupam poured her a peg of brandy from the decanter and made her take a sip. 'Be a good girl and drink this. You need it, Nalini.'

An hour later, Nalini washed her face, applied a fresh coat of make-up, and travelled a long distance alone. From Marine Drive to Pali Hills. Anupam switched on the table lamp and sat with a bunch of papers. He had a lecture next day at nine.

Several years later, Sureshwar informed that Maria's hat-making occupation was out of business. She had to visit a mental rehabilitation centre quite often. Maria never got over that nervous breakdown.

Why didn't you learn the art of self-defence, Maria? It was your life against mine. How would our lives shape up if I brought you to Calcutta? You might stay afloat. But I would be the one to drown. Life is tough, if you know what Darwin said about 'survival of the fittest'. Any battle implies that you have to fight against somebody. We cannot fight a battle if there is no one on the other side. We pit ourselves against each other in order to win.

If you want to avoid war, you have to go in exile. The society is a battleground, Maria. One side will lose out of the two. Some are born to be exploited, while some to be exploiters. Only the latter survive. But you belong to the community of survivors. When it comes to struggle, Jews know it better than everybody else. Why don't you have that skill? You are to blame because you are weak.

TWENTY-TWO

Feeling sleepy. Might fall asleep now. I am tired of battles. Who am I fighting? I am a soldier, undoubtedly. It is true that I use complex war tactics in my life. Something which Niru never does. Niru does not need to protect himself. He is not a Kshatriya*. I have to keep my armour on all the time. Guarding through days and nights without sleep is a price that a conqueror pays. Niru has never been out to conquer the world. He is happy in his family space. But who am I fighting? I am not that charming lunatic from La Manche*. My war is not against grass, horses, lambs, and windmills. Humans fight humans.

Anupam's peace-loving self was embarrassed at such thoughts. My charges are against the system, not against humans. Why am I being slain by so many enemies? This is not a fight to change the system; this is about being in a warlike state all the time. So, am I scared of someone? Who is it?

---

* One of the four social orders, the warrior class, of Vedic society.

* *The Ingenious Nobleman Sir Quixote of La Mancha* (Spanish: *El Ingenioso Hidalgo Don Quijote de la Mancha)* by Miguel de Cervantes was published in two volumes in 1605 and 1615. The story follows the adventures of a noble (hidalgo) named Alonso Quixano, who reads so many chivalric romances that he loses his sanity and decides to set out to revive chivalry, undo wrongs, and bring justice to the world, under the name *Don Quixote de la Mancha*.

Anupam's lips and hands craved for a cigarette. But Ma's hands on his hair reminded him of the doctor's warning.

The fist fight had started. Anupam, the question is, are you going to tighten your grip or let it loose?

The game is predesigned. Yet, try to make a humble effort. You better change your strategy. Your enemy is of a different make. Pride will not work, humility might. Where is that much-reputed intelligence of yours? '*Budhousharanamaniccha*'—apply your intelligence to keep it at arm's length. Do not use the same weapon on all enemies. There are different mantras for different gods. You cannot hunt down a tiger with a bird-killing catapult. New weapons for a new war. Cool down, Anupam. Look what you have inside your heart. Weapons, treasures ... look for the tree of knowledge you had planted in your childhood.

Ma, you have no formal education. You spent your entire life under Jethima's infinite authority. Yet, how easily you could say, 'Do not take up a job where your heart isn't.' How simply you said, 'You should not go against your values even to save your life.' Ma, where did you learn all these? I said, 'How can you stand Jethima?' And you replied so easily, 'She is unfortunate anyway. All her life she has been cheated. She never got to know how her husband cheated her. We should not hurt her.' My intelligence is of no value. I now realize that Jethima is the object of pity in the picture, not you. Where did you get these weapons of forgiveness, kindness, and patience? Ma, your Anu has done exactly what he was not supposed to do. He has sacrificed his conscience to save his petty life, not once but a number of times. Dear Ma, there is no end to my confusion and fears.

Please be kind to me, Samir, Somen, Dipu, Badal, Ashish. I do not even deserve your hatred. Forgive me, Maria, Nalini, Kamalkali, Menaka. I am coward and selfish.

Baba, my only way out is that I am your son. Blood? Will blood not do its job? Chromosomes? '*Api, chet, sudurocharo….*' Baba, do you remember that you used to say, '*Khiprong bhavati dharmatma saswat shanting nigacchati*?' Baba, this sinner is your son. Won't he be saved from destruction?

I will remove this dirty set of clothes and go for a holy dip in unstitched clothes just like you. Won't my sins get washed away in your purity?

Krishnachaitanya Bhattasharman, my late father, please listen to me. I pledge to start anew. I am yet to forget the star-studded sky you showed me. The Gayatri Mantra remains intact in my memory. I have torn off the sacred thread, but have I been able to do away with it?

I will sell off the flat in Camac Street. Just need to make a call in the evening. Baba, I will not go to that locality any more.

'*Ayamarambho shubhay bhavatu*'—let this beginning be an auspicious one.

Niru, the green kite of yours that I had torn, for which you had wept so hard, I cannot bring it back again.

'There's a call for you, Dadababu.'

Anupam's slumber was disturbed. Was he actually sleeping? Ma was not by his side. Did Ma come today?

'Ma urged not to call you, but they are saying that it is really important. It is Mr Dastur from some newspaper house.'

Anupam dragged himself to the telephone. Urgent! What could be the matter?

'Hello, Mr Dastur. Roy speaking. Yes?'

His mother sounded worried after he finished his call.

'What is it? Why was the call so important? Do not speak. Write it on the slate.'

Anupam wrote, 'Call Niru once.'

'What happened? Something wrong?' Ma asked while handing him the slate.

Anupam wrote, 'I am going to get an award. Magsaysay Award.* The amount is ten thousand dollars, which amounts to Rs. 75,000.

'Hare Krishna Hare Krishna, Krishna Krishna Hare Hare! Jai Radhamadav! God, you are kind.'

Anupam croaked in irritation, 'It is not about God; it is about diplomacy. Someone wanted to give the award to an Indian, so they chose me. I have no personal credit for this.'

'This is because of God's grace, son. There are so many people in India. Why did they choose my sick child? Anu, offer your prayers to your father. Jai Radhamadhav!'

---

* An annual award established to perpetuate former Philippine president Ramon Magsaysay's example of integrity in governance, courageous service to the people, and pragmatic idealism within a democratic society.

Anupam felt like touching his mother's feet. That would be a natural gesture under the grimy ceilings or within the damp walls of their house in Darjipara. Anupam wanted to do it and tried hard, but his limbs would not bend in this carpeted prison, which was plastic-painted in a tint of eggshell. His forehead was unable to touch the ground. Anupam wondered whether he could touch his mother's feet if it was his birthday, Vijaya Dashami, or Poila Boishakh. Anupam, why are you so ashamed to express humility when you come from a Vaishnava family? Why are you so hesitant to touch someone's feet? You said, '*ayamarambha shubhay*.' Imagine this day to be your birthday or Vijaya Dashami, Anupam. Why is it not the New Year's day?

Anupam called out to her, 'Ma!'

Belarani was about to leave the room. She turned back. Who was it touching her feet? 'Who is this? My Anu?'

TWENTY-THREE

Deus ex machina—when gods and goddesses descend from heaven on the stage to curse or bless, or to test the protagonist. Anupam smiled to himself at this thought. It is a divine prop used to rescue the protagonist from all evils. He had experienced this since childhood. The problem always gets solved in the end. However, to save himself, an alert Anupam had to control the pulley from behind the curtains. The Magsaysay Award is entering the stage as the greatest divine intervention in his life, but there were two major differences. First, this time, he was not the one responsible for pulling strings. There was someone else backstage. Ma would say that it was Radhamadhav, the divine magician of the Roy Mansion who could make a dumb man speak. He was standing behind the wings and roping in miracles with His love and grace. But Anupam knew that the real game was about random force. A few people were prone to accidents and a few were prone to good fortune. People who won in gambling won in love. They were gods' favourite; gods descended on earth to help them out. Anupam was one of those fortunate people. Life had always bowed down to him, and he was used to its special treatment. Thus, at this moment of crisis, receiving the bag of gold from Magsaysay did not surprise him.

Things were different this time, though. It was not clear whether he was fortunate or unfortunate to receive this award. There was something funny about it. The irony being that the award was named after Ramon Magsaysay. A person who was known for his radical right-wing views. Anupam himself wrote a lot on communist killings at one point of time. He recalled his essays now. Magsaysay! Money from Phillipines would mean ... Anupam, the Marxist political analyst, smiled to himself. Good, Anupam! The game is entirely different this time!

But this was not required.

Here was the difference. The money for treatment had been arranged and he had decided to sell off the flat at Camac Street. Why did the gods shower their blessings after the problem got resolved? What could this imply? But this meant that he might not need to sell the flat. So, was this the supernatural design? Sukumar Chakraborty's smirk proved to be ineffective then—he would not have to give up his flat. Just that? That simple? Or was there a deeper conspiracy beneath? It was still not clear whether the award was a blessing or a curse. Or was it a test?

Strange that this did not occur to him earlier. Anupam could see the true picture now. He did not need to be scared of Sukumar's scornful look after the world got to know that he was going to receive the Magsaysay Award. Even if he did not buy the flat now, his 'ability' would not be challenged. His potentials would soon be the talk of 'public knowledge'.

That meant he was out of it. Anupamkrishna Bhattasharman would not go back to Camelia Apartments. He would not go back to Roy Mansion either. He would continue to live in this simple Bengali middle-class neighbourhood. Maybe, one day again, the word 'taxi' would remind him of railway station or the hospital. Emergency?

He would give away the entire money of Magsaysay. The money from the flat would be enough for his surgery abroad.

Seventy-five thousand. He needed to find out whether the money was tax-free. In all probabilities, tax would not be deducted. If he still needed to give up a part of the award money as income tax, he would do so. As regards the rest of the amount, fifteen thousand would go for securing a bed in the government hospital for people like Maria, fifteen for providing legal aid to young political prisoners, fifteen to Mother Teresa for looking after women bearing illegitimate children, and fifteen for deaf and dumb schools. If he managed to save some money, he would donate it to the blind school.

Sensory control is a rare virtue, and sensory void a punishment. Animals do have senses. They have all the basic needs of life—sight, hearing, and speech. Lack of it spells disaster.

Where was Ajitnarayan now? Anupam did not get a chance to fulfil Ajitnarayan's basic needs.

A young man in tattered clothes and shoes approached him one day in Gariahat. His skin tone unrecognizable with mud and dirt, he glared at Anupam with his mucus-filled eyes, pointed his index finger at him, and asked, 'Anupam Roy? You can't recognize me?'

A surprised Anupam said, 'You are?'

'You don't know me. I have attended a lot of your lectures. But you do not come for any of my lectures. I am Ajitnarayan Choudhury,' he said in a British accent.

'Where? Where do you hold your lectures?'

'Ramkrishna Mission. Where else? No other auditorium in the world is as good. I am not Vivekananda that they will send me to Chicago. Do you think I will travel with CIA's money? No! Not me!' Ajitnarayan beat his frail chest and looked condescendingly at Anupam. As if he was looking down at Anupam from a seven-storeyed building. 'I am a solid person, totally honest. I will show you my articles. They have been published in Russia, USA, Brazil, New Guinea, Japan, and Korea ... where not? You gather all your material from my work and write your books. Yet,' Ajitnarayan pouted, 'you never acknowledge me in your papers.' Seeing his eyes welling up, Anupam hurriedly asked, 'So, where can I find your essays?'

'In the National Library. Don't even know that? Silly! You could also come home. Most welcome!'

Ajitnarayan pointed to the nearest high-rise, 'That's my residence. Every room is air-conditioned. But I don't know how to say it. Using the washroom is a hassle,' Ajitnarayan whispered in an intimate way. 'I cannot use it like uncivilized people. Can you please arrange for a flushing system? Don't you think every civilized person requires privacy and sanitary privy? Aren't these a cultivated individual's basic needs? I don't even have that!'

Anupam was embarrassed. Pedestrians around must be wondering why he was talking to a man who was stark, raving mad. He said 'achcha' to terminate the conversation and tried to walk away. Ajit ran and tugged at his shirt, 'Listen, I pay one thousand to my present PA. I will give you three thousand. You are appointed as my new assistant. You will look after my basic needs from today. Okay?'

'Fine, fine.' Anupam somehow freed his shirt from Ajit's grasp and escaped.

From then onwards, Anupam met Ajit every time he went to Gariahat. Ajit would say, 'PA, see the condition I am in. You are not fulfilling your duties. You are not ensuring that my basic needs are met with.'

One day he said, 'PA, please give me ten thousand rupees. I have to go on a continental trip. Have to discuss a few things with Russel and Sartre and get my brain insured. Just like Marlene Dietrich insured her legs with a million dollars. You will accompany me, PA. Where's the money?'

Anupam said, 'But trust me, Ajitbabu, forget ten thousand, I don't even have one rupee with me.'

'Okay. Give me two rupees for the time being.'

Anupam turned his pocket inside out to show that he had no money. Ajit looked at the prominent void. There was profuse empathy in his eyes.

'Poor Anupam. Even you are in this state? These are hard times. Wait, I shall help you.' He combed through the filthy rags on his body and brought out a note and few coins. He bought a packet of masala *muri** and tugged at Anupam's shirt, 'Please do not run away. Have something. How will your brain work otherwise?' He took a fistful and handed the packet to Anupam. Then he tucked the sweaty, reeking note into Anupam's equally sweaty hands and said, 'Keep it till you see better days.'

Ajitnarayan smiled sympathetically, showing his yellow teeth. Anupam could not bring himself to take that packet from Ajit. Ajit's fingers were blue with all the dirt and germs of the world. He requested humbly, 'Ajitbabu, my stomach is not keeping well. You have it, please!'

'Oho! This is the extent of your digestive capacity at such a young age! Look at me,' Ajit squatted on the footpath and stuffed the *muri* into his mouth with both hands. The *muri* spilled out of his mouth like broken teeth. With his mouth stuffed, Ajit kept laughing and waved his hand at him with great condescension, 'You may go now. Your services are no longer needed. You have failed.' Anupam walked towards him, trembling. He handed him the note that he was clutching fervently like the sandalwood-pasted holy leaves people offer to God, 'Take this. Keep it. I have money at home.'

'So? Why do you keep the money at home and come to office empty-handed? To beg, to borrow, and to steal? I will not take that money. Do you know that if you lend money and take it back, you are reborn as a dog in Kalighat? I am a laid-back person; I can't opt for a dog's life.'

---

* Puffed rice.

Laughing out freely, Ajit nonchalantly emptied the rest of the packet in Gariahat's crossing—as if setting free a flock of white birds. He derived a kind of pure pleasure from it. Pristine, white bits of puffed rice filled the hungry air of Gariahat. The rice numbed Anupam's senses for a few seconds with the fierceness of a hailstorm. It was impossible to return the money to Ajit.

The son of a poor widow, Ajit was studying English honours when he developed signs of insanity. His mother could not keep him at home. With a lot of sympathy bestowed upon him by the shop owners, Ajit became the sole monarch of Gariahat.

Soon after that incident, Anupam spoke to a doctor friend and arranged to get Ajit admitted to Lumbini Hospital. To fulfil his 'basic needs'—'privacy' and 'sanitary privy'. But, just after that, Ajit disappeared from Gariahat altogether. Leaving Anupam Roy indebted, even if for a rupee. It was probably his first defeat.

Since then, Anupam got nervous whenever he saw deranged people. He searched. Was it Ajit, his creditor? What was he saying? 'It's a dog's life. I have some basic needs.'

He could not talk, but his mind was talking incessantly. Not having money for the surgery was a concern. Now he had far more money than necessary. That was a worse problem. His life would be miserable after the news was out in the newspapers and radio—he would be flooded with good wishes from the public. Just now, when he was strictly forbidden to speak! People who wanted to shower attention on him would return hurt and insulted. Anupam, why are you bothered with things that are no longer in your control? Don't waste your time. In fact, there is a way out. Publish a note in the newspaper, explaining and apologizing for the inconvenience caused. That should do.

A to-do list must be prepared. He would have to make arrangements for his travel. He was not supposed to talk for three weeks now, after which he would leave for Vienna. What are the things to be arranged? Anupam, concentrate. Where is your sense of discipline? *'Bandhuraatman jenataibatna jito'*—one who has control over oneself, wins. Calm yourself. Put all thoughts away. Think about your work. What should you work on now?

TWENTY-FOUR

There was a divine, enriched darkness. Even though it was midday, the curtains were drawn in, making the room as still and desolate as midnight.

Keshto was not supposed to call him for visitors. He was copying everybody's details in a notebook. Anupam would write to them in response. But not a word. With every sentence, with every word, the life of his vocal chords was dying out. As Dr Roychoudhury had strictly mentioned, his treatment would be useless if he did not allow his larynx complete rest.

Anupam was lying on his mother's favourite armchair, his right hand resting lifeless on the armrest, and his left hand folded over his eyes. The to-do list was ready in his mind. He just needed to put it down in the notebook: 1. Reserve Bank 2. Air India 3. Visa form 4. Medical certificate 5. Leave application 6. No-objection letter 7. Inform All India Radio that 'Roy's Corner' would be going off-air until further notice (until his voice returned).

Until further notice? What if his voice was never cured? What if his voice never returned? ... What if ... what if something more did not return?

It was not improbable. The doctors might find some other problem while performing the surgery on him. Something worse than what they had been expecting. There was no guarantee that the operation would be carried out without any obstacles—simply and successfully. There was a 20 per cent risk in all operations. Some do not regain consciousness from the anesthesia, while, for some, the blood pressure falls suddenly. They do not come back alive from the operation table.

In case there was a blood clot rushing towards your heart, the doctors could hardly do anything to prevent it. Plus, there was always a greater chance of being diagnosed with something else during the surgery. You have not been tested for malignancy, Anupam.

Who knows what terrible surprise, enmity, or shock was waiting to pounce on him? Anupam, you are fighting against nature. You are fighting a non-human force. Intelligence is not even a weapon here. Anupam visualized a scene from an old film—a king playing chess with death. Anupam, you have not learnt this game, you see.

What if only his middle-aged, tired body came out of the operation theatre? A redundant body covered with a sheet from head to toe? Who would take charge of that desolate body in a foreign land?

Surrounded by strangers, he might have to spend an uncertain amount of time inside a freezer which was not suitable for life—the once known Anupam K. Roy, who would have lost his present and would have no future. His lifeless body would have to wait until the honourable

Indian embassy was kind enough to arrange for its return. Impersonal and legal.

Anupam could see the interiors of a huge, white building. Labyrinthine corridors, with ceilings, walls, and floors the colour of seashells ... so gleaming white that even one's shadow would not be reflected on them. No doors. A solitary body wrapped in a white sheet from head to toe, moving through every turn and corner of the corridor. A pleasant silence shrouding the expanse of the silvery corridor. The air still and heavy with emptiness; the smell of antiseptics in the air getting heavier and heavier and squeezing out all the oxygen until it was suffocating. Suddenly, there was a sound of a pair of running feet—it was rising, echoing through the trapped air, and gradually turning into a deafening noise. Anupam was covering both his ears—trying to scream—his stupor broke as the sweat from his hands got into his heated ears.

How impossibly hot! As if there was a fire inside his skull. Oh, what a terrible daydream! Anupam, why are you harbouring such morbid thoughts? Why would you think of death before undergoing a normal surgery? Are you scared? Anxious? Decay? Loss? Pain? Control all your emotions, as a tortoise controls its whole body by going into the shell. Just as the flame of a lamp does not flicker when there is no wind, you too be still. Don't be driven by the wind, Anupam. Remember, *'bondhuratmanamannstasya'*—he who has control over himself ...

But, would he have to go into the operation theatre alone? Would there be no one walking restlessly outside the OT, anxious for him?

Ma would be taking refuge at the feet of Lord Radhamadhav in their house in Darjipara. And Niru? O, goodness! He was so distraught when Bithi was about to give birth to their child. The doctor could not decipher whether the father was experiencing labour pain or the mother. He could not depend upon him during crises. Then? Did that mean there would be no one with him by his hospital bed in that foreign land? What if there was no recovery? Every major operation had some element of risk involved.

Anupam, look at yourself! Sick thoughts are hovering around your mind as the stray dogs that run to the nearest rubbish dump. Willpower is the only way to drive away morbid thoughts. Try it, '*sarbatrarani sangjamaya manorhidi nirudha ca*'—control your emotion and your mind, harbour healthy thoughts. It is within your power. Think of more useful things. Don't allow yourself useless indulgences.

The other Anupam smirked. Contemplating death is horrifying, but not recognizing when it stands in front of you? Is it natural? Is that a healthy thought? Sudha had said, 'One should be ready to face all kinds of truth.' All those are your silly antics to avoid the reality. '*Jatasya hi dhruvamrityu*'—if you are born, you must die. That's scientific truth.

He remembered the tale of Theseus. I, too, need a ball of thread. Without that, I will not enter the labyrinth of corridors in Vienna. It will not be prudent. Baba, please forgive me. I have been a coward. I have been restless and covetous. And I have failed. Right from my childhood, I used to think that Jyathamoshai is the ideal, intelligent man. But that ball of thread is finished now.

I want another ball of thread now. I have enough weapons to face Minotaur, but what is the next step? Who will help me find my way home? You tell me, Baba, is it wise to get into a maze without knowing the way out? You could manage to find your way back; the sacred thread on your body would provide you the clue.

I threw away the reel of thread you gave me. I did that in my childhood. Will it return to my hands again? I have to resolve this problem myself. This is my actual thread ceremony, Baba. I will come of age now.

TWENTY-FIVE

Trapped inside Anupam Roy's neat, smart, closed-door, and curtained interiors, midday looked as helpless as midnight.

He put his feet on the stool and reclined on the chair. His eyelids were locked by his well-built, strong, bronzed arms. The other hand lay motionless on the armrest.

He imagined walking up to the chest of drawers, taking out his airmail pad, and opening his favourite pen named after a mountain peak. But his eyelids did not open, his hands were static, and his body lay still like the other furniture in the room.

Only his lips moved. They fluttered under the shadow of his thin, manly moustache. His life trembled softly in the manner of a person whispering a prayer in secret, surrendering ... Anupam started drafting a letter without a pen and a paper:

Sudha,

Don't be surprised thinking that this is a response to your letter. How are you, Sudha? I am not keeping well.

Next month, I will be undergoing a surgery in Vienna. It is a trivial matter. After the surgery, I might get my voice back, or maybe not. I can't talk, Sudha, even now. Did I ever know how to talk? I may pick up the skill later, or maybe not. I might not need to do that at all. In case there are complications and I do not come back, someone needs to bring back whatever remains.

Sudha, will you bring me back if I lose my way? Don't say no, Sudha. Anupam is lonely. He does not have dreams; he does not have anything at all. Sudha, are you listening? I have to come back even if I lose my way. Please be with me. Don't leave me. Sudha, can you recognize me? I am Anupam.

Sudha, this is not a reply to the letter that you wrote. This is just my letter.

Dhur, does anyone write a letter like this? Can a letter like this be written? No it can't be. *Babah*, I can't do this. Give me another spool of thread. Not Sudha.

The other Anupam said, 'There's no one. No one else. No other way out except Sudha. Only Sudha.'

What's it ... Who is it? Who's there?

Anupam was alarmed. Did someone knock at the door amidst this tremulous silence?

Anupam listened with baited breath. Yes, there was a knock.

Once, twice, thrice.

Silence followed after three knocks. Anupam counted. Three more knocks now. His unbearable loneliness that filled him to the brim spilled out with force.

'Who is it!' Anupam screamed his lungs out in his already damaged voice.

'It's me. I brought tea,' Keshto replied in astonishment. 'Can I come in?'

'Oh!' It was as if Anupam woke up from a trance. He replied softly, 'It's open, come in.'

'Did you fall asleep?' Keshto asked as he kept the tea tray on the table.

'No.'

'Then? Were you working?'

'No. Why?'

'I called you for a long time. There was no response.'

Anupam answered painfully, 'Keshto, I did not hear.'

'No, don't talk. It is okay. I was wondering what could have happened … ' an embarrassed Keshto replied.

Keshto wanted to change the topic of discussion. So he started pulling the curtains back with sudden promptness. 'I am opening the shutters; the light has faded. The evening breeze is already blowing.'

The sky encroached upon the room in a moment. Anupam was scorched by the blaze of the evening sun. Even Keshto's eyes were dazzled by this unearthly fire. The setting sun had set Anupam's hair, forehead, jaw, and nose ablaze. Anupam's face glistened like a new bronze sculpture. The alien glow on the divine form appeared unworldly.

The sight of Anupam knotted up Keshto's nerves. He looked bedazzled. He tried to run away, but suddenly noticed Anupam's face in an earthly light. On the tired, exhausted skin shone glistening beads of sweat.

In the corner of his carefully pressed eyes, age had played tic-tac-toe. His forehead was like a beach with furrows running like millions of fine lines made by the silent movement of crabs. The evening stubble on his cheeks resembled dots of sandalwood paste. And a depressing fold of skin ran from his nose to his mouth like a wound—his lips were quivering like a child talking in his sleep—was he melancholic or satisfied?

Keshto bent down and, like handling expensive bone china, called out carefully, very softly, 'Dadababu?'

There was no response. Keshto waited for some time and left the room in silence.

The evening breeze swept across the room through the open windows and fluttered through Anupam's flesh and bones with ease, as usual.

***